Of Dragons and Stone

OF DRAGONS AND STONE

A COMPANION TO
MOUNTAIN OF DRAGONS AND SACRIFICE

LCCN: 2024918619

ISBN: 978-1-943442-59-1

Author's Note

While much of this novella takes place before the events of *Mountain of Dragons and Sacrifice*, *Of Dragons and Stone* is best read after that book. There are spoilers for *Mountains of Dragons and Stone* in this book.

Night of the Dragon Steward

Prologue

Six-year-old Dorrian huddled against the wall, rubbing his arms and shivering in the cold air that flowed around the huge cavern. The rags he wore were a pitiful excuse for clothing, doing little to warm him. His bare feet shifted against the gritty stone floor.

Around him, other fae from the Court of Sand clustered. Some weeping. Some defiant. All of them casting glances at the four dragons of Flight Icewing only a few feet away.

Their captors.

Two of the Icewing dragons were in half-dragon form with fae bodies and ice-gray wings rising from their backs. The other two lounged in full dragon form, one with eyes half-closed as if dozing while the other tore at a hunk of beef, slurping down the meat and licking his chops in a way that sent shivers down Dorrian's spine.

Well, more shivers.

He tried to make himself look smaller as he took in the cavern bustling with dragons, both in half-dragon form and as massive dragons with wings and scales and mouths big enough to swallow him in one gulp.

Were he and the others here to be eaten? Perhaps Flight Icewing had brought the captives from their war in the Court of Sand here as an appetizer.

Dorrian sniffed and scrubbed at his face. He wanted to go home. He wanted his papa and mama. He wanted things to go back to the way they were, before the attacks from the Realm of Monsters and before the king of the Court of Sand had made a bargain with Flight Icewing...only to break that bargain and incur the dragons' wrath. So many had died, including Dorrian's parents.

He was alone. Hungry. Cold. Probably about to be eaten.

The feasting and talking of the gathered dragons seemed to go on and on. Occasionally, a dragon would step into the center and make a booming proclamation in a way that would make the other dragons stop what they were doing and listen for a while before they went back to eating and talking.

A fifth dragon from Flight Icewing strode up to them in half-dragon form, tipping his head scornfully at Dorrian and the others. "Get them up."

The other four dragons poked and prodded and herded them toward the center of the cavern. Dorrian stumbled along with the others, blinking out at the crowd of dragons. Most looked scary, their eyes glittering, their fangs flashing bright in the candlelight.

The fifth dragon climbed onto the huge stone in the

center of the room, blurring into his full dragon form. His voice booming, he spoke of battles and victories and lots of things Dorrian didn't fully understand. At the end of it, he gestured to Dorrian and the others. "I've brought with me captives from the Court of Sand who stand ready to bind themselves in service to a dragon. What will you bargain for their pledges of service?"

There was a stir of murmuring among the closest dragons. A few stepped forward, shouting out offers and pointing at some of the captives.

A dragon with brown hair and royal blue wings rising from his back stepped forward. Something about his slim shoulders and gangling frame made him seem younger than the others. This dragon gestured at Dorrian. "It's against the laws of the Fae Realm to bargain with children. This one is below the age of majority, too young to bind himself in service."

"And you, Evander of Flight Clawstone, are barely old enough to speak in these halls." The dragon of Flight Icewing sneered down at the young half-dragon before his gaze flicked to an older dragon who was hurrying through the crowd of dragons. "Rockenthar, control your spawn."

The older dragon, his brown hair and blue wings a similar shade to the younger one, rested a hand on his shoulder. "No need when my son speaks the truth."

"There are exceptions for orphans who have no guardians to speak for them in cases such as this." The Icewing dragon snorted a puff of smoke. "Now either bargain for him or cease speaking."

"I'll bargain for him." A half-dragon with an especially sharp face and bright green wings stepped forward. The glitter in his eyes matched the flash of his far too sharp teeth as he smiled the kind of smile that had Dorrian shrinking back. "I find the young ones are the most trainable."

"Not so fast." The younger, blue-winged dragon stepped forward. "I began bargaining first, so that gives me first claim."

Dorrian hunched his shoulders as he tried to follow the bargaining, his stomach twisting. He didn't like the look in the green-winged dragon's eyes.

Would the blue-winged dragon, the one called Evander, be any better?

In the end, it was Evander who took Dorrian's hand and tugged him away from the others.

When they were free of the mass of dragons gathered around the center stone, Evander halted, though he didn't let go of Dorrian's hand.

Dorrian blinked, his eyes blurring. But he gasped his tears away, keeping them silent. He'd gotten very good at crying silently.

The older blue-winged dragon clapped the younger one on the shoulder. "I'm proud of you, Evander. Though, I would've thought you already had enough on your talons with your maiden problem."

Evander shrugged. "I couldn't leave him there."

"I would have claimed him if you hadn't." The older dragon gestured toward Dorrian, though he kept his gaze on Evander. "Would you like me and your mother to look after him?"

Evander shook his head. "I'll take him back to my eyrie. Phoebe will look after him, if he truly doesn't have any family left."

The other dragon nodded. "Go on then. I'll stay and finish up here. There might be a few of the others I can bargain to free. Disgusting practice."

Evander grimaced, then his gaze swung down to Dorrian.

Dorrian quailed, hurriedly scrubbing at his face with his sleeve. The other dragons hadn't liked it when any of them cried.

As the older dragon spun on his heel and strode away, Evander knelt, putting his amber-blue dragon-eyes level with Dorrian's face. "You don't have to be scared of me, all right?"

Dorrian sniffed, trying and failing to stop his shivering, both from fear and the cold. It was rather hard not to be scared of a dragon.

Evander reached into a pocket and pulled out a truly massive blanket. He wrapped it around Dorrian's shoulders, most of the blanket piling on the floor at Dorrian's feet. "I'm going to take you to my home. My housekeeper Phoebe will look after you. She's really nice. Is that all right with you?"

Why was the dragon asking him? From his short experience, dragons didn't ask before they did stuff.

Dorrian rubbed his running nose on the blanket. The blanket was soft and warm and nice. Maybe this dragon was nice too. He seemed less scary than the others. "Will there be food?"

"Yes, lots of food. Are you hungry?" Evander reached into his pocket again.

Dorrian nodded, hunching his shoulders. "Those other dragons didn't give us food."

"You haven't eaten since you were taken from the

Court of Sand?" Evander pulled what looked like a piece of pink bread out of his pocket. "Looks like this is all I have left. Here, you can have it. There will be more food at my eyrie."

Holding the blanket with one hand, Dorrian snatched the piece of bread, stuffing most of it in his mouth before the dragon could take it away.

"I'm going to pick you up, if that's all right?" Evander remained kneeling before Dorrian.

Dorrian nodded again, tugging the blanket tight around him. At least if he went with this nice dragon, he could leave this cavern filled with lots of scary ones.

Evander stood, then picked Dorrian up, blanket and all.

Dorrian curled in the dragon's arms, shoving the last of the bread in his mouth. His papa used to carry him like this when they had to run from the monsters and Dorrian got too tired to keep running. Dorrian had always felt so safe in his papa's arms.

Until the day they hadn't been able to run fast enough, and Dorrian had been left alone.

Evander strode into another one of the dark tunnels, his footsteps echoing off all the stone around them. "What's your name?"

"Dorrian," Dorrian mumbled into the blanket, leaning his head against the dragon's chest. So tired. Still kind of hungry.

At least he wasn't cold anymore.

"Do you have any family back in the Court of Sand?"

Dorrian shook his head. "The monsters got them."

"I'm so sorry." Evander's arms tightened around him in something almost like a hug. "Well, you're going to have a new family now, if you want it. Or I'll find you a new home in the Court of Sand. Either way, I'm going to free you from the captive binding. I'm not going to force you to pledge yourself to me or anything like that."

Dorrian just nodded yet again, not sure what that all meant. But it sounded nice. Much better than the stuff the scary dragons had been saying.

He closed his eyes, snuggled deeper into the blanket, and drifted off to sleep, safer than he'd been in a long time.

Chapter One

TWENTY-THREE YEARS LATER

Dorrian sauntered down the passageway from his room in the mountain eyrie and into the large space that provided an eating and gathering area for all those who lived here. A large fireplace dominated one side, low embers still burning and heating the space. The long banks of windows showed the gray dark of early morning, the first glints lighting the tips of the distant mountains.

Long tables and benches filled most of the space while a rug and a few chairs clustered before a fireplace. At this time of the morning, all the benches and chairs were empty.

Savory smells wafted from the nook on one side of the room that formed the kitchen space. Candles blazed, pooling light into the rest of the room, while Phoebe bustled between the stove and the worktable.

Dressed in a simple gown with an apron over it,

Phoebe wore her dark hair piled on her head, no strands of gray amid the curls. As Dorrian crossed the room and entered the kitchen, she glanced at him, a smile creasing her cheeks and crinkling the skin by her eyes. "Good morning, Dorrian. Getting an early start, I see."

"Hoping to get somewhat caught up before Evander wakes." Dorrian reached for one of the freshly baked pink biscuits. He popped a bite in his mouth, chewing the sweet, soft bread. "Good morning."

He was always an early riser. Which worked well, as Evander tended to be a night dragon who preferred to wait to rise until the sun was up. Dorrian took full advantage of those hours of quiet in the morning, and he especially enjoyed these few moments with just him and Phoebe before the others woke. She was something between a foster mother and a much older big sister, having all but raised him after he was brought to the eyrie.

As Evander had promised, he'd freed Dorrian from the captive binding. Although Dorrian had the option to return to the Court of Sand or go anywhere else in the Fae Realm, he'd chosen to remain here in the eyrie, serving Evander as a full member of the Court of Stone rather than bound the way other dragons bound their servants.

As Evander's steward, Dorrian had traveled back to the dragons' meeting hall several times over the years, lingering near the wall with the other stewards and servants, most of them bound to their dragons far more tightly than Dorrian was. They had spoken of the preserving magic that settled over the things a dragon chose to hoard, a magic that often extended to a dragon's hoard of bound servants.

They'd doubted Dorrian would experience this *preservation*, as he wasn't bound to Evander. But it seemed those servants had been wrong, not recognizing the strength found in bonds of friendship and brotherhood.

If the way Phoebe was nearing sixty by human years, and yet appeared far younger, was anything to go by then Dorrian, too, would find himself rather *well-preserved* as Evander's steward. He was likely already experiencing it, though at twenty-nine, the effect was that he was more a vague, twenty-something-ish age in the way Phoebe was preserved at an indeterminate middle-age.

Phoebe piled more of the biscuits, some eggs, and sausage on a tray, then held it out to him. "Then get on with you, now."

Dorrian took the tray, giving her a smile, before he strolled from the room.

Only a few of the torches still burned, low and guttering, at this time of early morning. But the ones that remained provided enough light for him to navigate the passageway from the kitchen to the large, central cavern. Here, a waterfall cascaded from above through an opening in the mountain, providing a glimpse of the dawn gray sky above.

Dorrian skirted the pool at the base of the waterfall, then strode up the broad staircase that led upward into the mountain. At the top, three doors stood around a small landing.

One led to the room where Evander kept his hoard

of rocks. The room straight ahead was Evander's bedchamber while the room to the right was the study.

Dorrian eased the door to the study open, tiptoed inside, and shut it quietly behind him so that he didn't wake Evander.

Inside, papers scattered over the desk and onto the floor. The cubby on the far side of the room that magically received messages from all over the Fae Realm was so stuffed with parchments and scrolls that several had overflowed onto the floor.

Dorrian shook his head, set the tray on the one cleared corner of the desk, lit a lamp, and set to work transforming the mess Evander had made of the room the night before after Dorrian had finished for the day. He ate his breakfast between sorting through all the parchments, scrolls, ledgers, and books scattered around the room.

He held his quill in his left hand, working extra hard to write without smudging the words with the side of his hand. The last thing he wanted was smudged records.

There were reports from the gem polishers of what they'd finished throughout the day, the quality of the gems, and where the gems had been sent. Dorrian reviewed those reports, made notes in a ledger, and stacked those parchments for filing in the store room.

He reviewed the stacks and stacks of requests for gems from other fae courts, taking notes on what gems were needed so that he could provide both the gem polishers and the mining gnomes a list of what gems to watch for and where to send them.

Another complaint from the Court of Revels. One of

the noble ladies this time instead of their queen, but still irritating. He added it to the pile of correspondence that required a response.

Then…he halted over the next folded missive he pulled from the cubby. This one was from Evander's parents.

Dorrian set that paper next to the breakfast tray and his leftovers. Evander was sure to see it first thing there.

As the sun rose above the distant peaks, sunbeams falling through the windows and warming Dorrian's back, the study door opened, and Evander strode inside.

In the years since Evander had rescued Dorrian, he'd filled out into an adult with broad shoulders and a sense of power that clung to his bearing. Now that Dorrian had grown, they were more or less the same age, and they had become more friends and brothers than young dragon and the scared boy he'd rescued.

Evander's gaze went straight to the tray with Dorrian's leftovers, a glint of hunger in his blue eyes despite the fact that he had surely eaten breakfast already.

Dorrian nudged the tray toward him. "Everyone thinks dragons are great predators, but you're really just scavengers."

Evander snorted and reached for one of the sausages Dorrian hadn't eaten. "We dragons can't help it if we burn through food so fast we're nearly always hungry."

Dorrian kept his grin from wavering. While it had been over twenty years since he'd known gnawing hunger, he could never quite forget what it felt like to be always hungry.

But instead of mentioning that, he rolled his eyes.

"Such a terrible price you pay for the ability to fly and breathe fire."

Evander shrugged, as if he didn't have a good comeback for that one. He reached for another of the sausages, sweeping a gaze over the room as if debating what to mess up first.

Dorrian pointed to the parchment he'd set next to the tray. "There's a message from your father."

Evander licked the grease from his fingers, then picked up the parchment. After breaking the seal and unfolding it, he read it quickly, a frown tugging down his mouth and his brows. "The leaders of Flight Clawstone have called a meeting, and my father wants me to attend. Some problems with Flight Raveneye."

"When is the meeting?" Dorrian halted his perusal of gem mining numbers, stomach sinking at the look on Evander's face.

"Tomorrow. My father wants me to leave today so we can discuss the political situation before the meeting." Evander lowered the parchment, meeting Dorrian's gaze.

"But you can't leave. The next maiden is going to be left any day now." Dorrian blinked at Evander, frozen where he sat.

"I know. I know." Evander gripped the parchment in a fist, wrinkling the paper as he paced before the desk.

Evander's "maiden problem" turned out to be a village of humans who had taken it into their heads to sacrifice a maiden to Evander each year. Despite Evander's best efforts to halt the sacrifices, the village kept doing it, leaving Evander little choice but to take the maidens back to the eyrie before they froze to death, were eaten by wolves, or were killed by their own village elders for being an unacceptable sacrifice.

The maidens were often terrified, fearing Evander would eat them or do something else terrible to them. They'd been taught by their village to believe that horrible wrath would be poured out on them and the village if they so much as looked on the dragon's face. It took weeks to even months of patience from Evander, Phoebe, Dorrian, and everyone here in the eyrie before the maidens were ready to build new lives for themselves.

Phoebe herself had been one of those sacrificed maidens, years before Dorrian had been brought to the eyrie. She was the only one who'd chosen to remain at the eyrie itself, though several had chosen to find a home for themselves in the fae village rather than return to the Human Realm.

Finally, Evander stopped pacing and faced Dorrian. "If the maiden is left while I'm gone, you'll have to fetch her."

"Me?" Dorrian rocked back in the chair, nearly tipping it over.

Evander held this duty close. He'd never entrusted it to anyone else before, not even Dorrian.

"Yes. We don't have much of a choice." Evander scrubbed his hand over his jaw before he held Dorrian's gaze. "Just be careful. The forest around the circle is rife with wolves, and the girls themselves are always terrified. There's a good chance she will lash out and hurt either you or herself in the process."

Dorrian nodded, swallowing. "I'll be careful."

He remembered all too well that night a few years

17

ago when Evander had flown back, a dagger in his chest, blood soaking his shirt, and a maiden shouting expletives locked away in a room. If Dorrian had been in Evander's place that night, he likely would have died. That girl, too, probably would have died, alone in the forest with nothing but a knife for protection.

"Hopefully it won't come to that, and I'll be back in time." Evander heaved a sigh and glared at the parchment in his hand. "But if I'm not, someone needs to rescue the poor girl before she's harmed."

Knowing dragon politics as Dorrian did, whatever situation had come up wouldn't be dealt with easily or quickly.

"I won't let you down." Dorrian's fingers clenched around the quill pen in his hand. This was not a responsibility he took on lightly. If he messed up and the maiden was hurt, Evander would take on the guilt as his own.

"I know you won't." Evander strode around the desk to clap Dorrian on the shoulder. "You never do."

DORRIAN BOLTED UPRIGHT IN BED, his room cloaked in black around him. What had woken him?

A piercing chime rang from the stone all around him.

The alert. Another maiden had been left on the stone in the faerie circle down the mountain.

Dorrian rolled out of bed, hurriedly dressing in his warmest clothing. He raced down the corridor to the kitchens, finding Phoebe there, piling items on the worktable. Dorrian glanced around, his heart sinking. "Evander hasn't returned yet?"

It had been a faint hope that Evander had flown back into the eyrie in the few hours since Dorrian went to bed.

Phoebe shook her head. "No. I'm afraid it's up to you this time, Dorrian."

Dorrian braced his hands against the worktable, dragging in deep breaths to steady himself. Then he raised his head, taking in the pile on the table. "What is all this?"

"You aren't a dragon. The girl is going to have a long, cold walk back to the eyrie." Phoebe shoved a bundle of clothing items at him. "Here's some of my warm clothing she can borrow. Along with a few blankets."

Right. Until the eyrie had a maiden to provide for, the wardrobe in the room wouldn't produce any boots or cloaks for the poor girl who was even now shivering, tied to a stone wearing nothing but a sheer purple dress.

Dorrian stuffed the items into his magical pocket, then felt around in the pocket until his fingers brushed the hilt of the sword he had stashed in the pocket. He'd rarely had to use the sword he'd purchased at a fae market years ago, but having a weapon with him always steadied him, as if he could prevent a tragedy merely by being armed.

Phoebe held out a stoppered jug. "Some hot soup to warm her."

Dorrian nodded and stowed both the jug and two ceramic sipping bowls in his pocket as well. The magical space was filling quickly, but he still had room for a few more items if necessary.

Phoebe handed him a tin of balm, bandages, a lantern, and a means to light it. "I'll have the fire going in her room by the time you return. With Evander gone, there's no need to worry about too much light."

Dorrian drew his own cloak over his shoulders, nodding. "I'll be back as quickly as possible, but don't wait up for us. I can wake you once we arrive."

Phoebe came around the table, resting her hand briefly on his cheek, before she left the kitchen.

Dorrian took one last moment to make sure he had everything stowed in his magical pocket before he, too, strode from the kitchens. He turned left down a different passageway, a cold breeze wafting from ahead.

Time to rescue whatever poor girl had been left to die in the forest.

Chapter Two

Clarissa yanked on the rope tying her hands above her head, her sob catching in her throat.

This day had been one long, agonizing nightmare from the moment the head village elder announced her name. Being dragged into the citadel. Warned of her duty by the head elder's wife. Not being allowed to so much as hug her parents, her little sisters, and her best friend Nessa as the farewells were exchanged under the watchful eyes of the village elders.

Soon, this day would end in the worst nightmare of all. The dragon would swoop down, open his toothy maw, and…and…

Clarissa choked on a sob and yanked harder. Pain throbbed at her wrists as her skin tore, but the ropes didn't budge.

The stone beneath her leached the warmth from her body. A shiver of cold joined her shuddering fear. How long would it be now? She'd been shivering on this stone for what felt like hours, though it could have only been minutes.

The time dragged, the stars circling overhead. The moon rose, and that sent another round of shakes through her. The head village elder hadn't blindfolded her, but he'd warned her to keep her eyes shut if the dragon didn't arrive before moonrise.

What did it mean that the dragon wasn't here yet? Had Clarissa managed to do something wrong and she didn't even know it? Would the dragon refuse her as a sacrifice and burn the village anyway?

A long, lugubrious howl rose from farther up the mountain, the sound drifting on the frigid wind.

More howls joined the first, echoing off the evergreens around her.

Clarissa gasped, more sobs welling painfully in her chest even as she clamped her mouth shut on them. If she cried, would the wolves think her tears were the cries of a wounded animal?

She yanked on her bonds, her fingers and toes completely numb.

The howls continued, on and off, for what seemed like hours. Ever closer. Skittering prickles of fear over her skin.

Then the howls stopped. A shape moved in the darkness. Then another.

Clarissa couldn't stop the sob this time, her heart hammering hard and loud in her ears.

A wolf stepped from the shadows, head high, sniffing. It took a step, then retreated.

Another crept forward, hesitant and yet with eyes gleaming, teeth bared.

"Go away!" Clarissa shouted, trying to put as much fearless bravado into the words as she could. She'd always heard that wild animals were more scared of people than people were of them.

The wolves flinched away, darting back into the shadows. But they didn't leave, milling beneath the evergreens as if working up their courage to investigate whether she was foe or food.

"Go! Leave!" She screamed at them, but perhaps her voice was too shrill. Too much the panicked cry of a helpless creature rather than something the wolves should fear.

Growls came from the shadows. Wolves slunk forward, and this time when she yelled, they didn't back away.

The dragon had better get here soon, or she was going to be eaten by wolves.

What was she thinking? She'd end up eaten no matter what.

She sobbed, flinching as one wolf crept all the way up to the stone and sniffed her leg, its nose wet and cold against her skin. She kicked her leg as much as she could with her ankles tied to each other and the stone, and the wolf flinched back, retreating only a few steps.

The wolves would be on her in minutes. They were assessing her, seeing that despite her yells and wiggles, she wasn't running. She wasn't fighting. She was an easy meal, laid out on a platter for them.

Clarissa squeezed her eyes shut, her breaths hard and fast, her heart thrumming as if trying to beat out the last years of her life in seconds.

Something crashed in the brush. A yell. A person, not a wolf.

Clarissa's eyes snapped open, her eyelashes rimed in ice from her tears.

The dark silhouette of a man raced from between two of the evergreens, a gleaming sword in one hand, a lantern in the other. He yelled some kind of wordless battle cry as he charged the wolves, swinging the sword as if he meant to lop their heads off.

The wolves yipped and darted away, though they didn't go far.

The man brandished his sword and charged them again, giving that war cry.

This time, the wolves dashed away, disappearing beneath the trees.

The man stood there for a few minutes, his back to her, as he scanned the trees, holding the lantern high.

Then his shoulders relaxed, and he began to swing toward her. "I think the wolves are gone. For now, at least."

Clarissa squeezed her eyes shut before the lamp or the moonlight fully revealed the stranger's face to her. "Are you the dragon?"

"No." His voice held a huff of a laugh. "If I were the dragon, I would have roared and breathed fire at the wolves instead of charging them with a sword."

He had a good point. If he'd been the dragon, the wolves would've run in terror as soon as he arrived, sensing the presence of a superior predator.

Besides, he didn't have wings. While the village elders spoke about the dragon as if he was a bit more person-like than the depictions of him as a large, scaled creature would suggest, it still seemed like the dragon would have a few dragon-like qualities about him that would make him recognizable.

Clarissa peeled her eyes back open, her eyelashes threatening to freeze shut.

The man was facing her, his head bent as he stowed the sword at his side, the gleaming blade disappearing. A sheath at his side, most likely, something she wouldn't be able to see in the darkness of the cloak swathing his figure. Shadows highlighted his brows and the curve of his jaw, the lantern light shining against hair that appeared black in the night.

He set the lamp on the stone near her hands. "I'm sorry for the wait. It was a longer walk than I remembered. But I'm here now to rescue you."

Rescue. Such a thing hardly seemed possible.

The tension she'd been holding all day seeped away from her. She shuddered. So cold. So shaky.

But not dead. She didn't care who this stranger was. As long as he saved her from being eaten, she'd go anywhere with him.

DORRIAN TORE his gaze away from the girl's wide, terror-stricken eyes. Not that he could blame her, given the way he'd found her surrounded by wolves.

He reached into a pocket, drew out a knife, then set to work freeing her feet, then her hands.

Her lips were blue, her fingers and toes too. Her long dark brown hair straggled about her head, frozen to the stone below her in places. The flimsy material of

25

her dress also stuck to the stone, frozen in stiff folds around the girl.

As he freed her, her shaking worsened, her teeth chattering. She curled on her side, as if lacking the strength to sit up.

He dropped the knife into his pocket, then drew out the blankets. "Let's get you warm."

She didn't even nod or otherwise respond through her violent shivering. At least the shivering was a good sign. She wasn't so far gone that her body had stopped fighting the cold.

He tugged her into a sitting position, wrapping first one blanket, then the other, around her. She slowly curled her fingers in the blankets, weakly drawing them around her, even as her violent shaking continued.

The blankets wouldn't be enough.

Dorrian sat on the stone next to her, half-turning toward her. "Apologies for this, but you need to get warm."

The girl just blinked back at him, her eyes still a little unfocused, her expression still frozen in that numb, blank shock.

He gathered her into his arms, then drew her onto his lap. She made only a low whine of protest, her body stiff for only a moment before she sagged into him, as if her body's instinct for warmth overrode any other warring instincts at finding herself wrapped in a stranger's arms.

He wrapped his cloak around the two of them, tucking her feet against his side underneath his arm, her toes icy even through the layer of his shirt. The poor girl was folded up tightly to fit in his lap, her knees all the way to her chin.

For a second or two, she remained there, just a shivering, quaking form in his arms. Then, as if realizing just how warm he was, she snuggled into his arms, tucking her head beneath his chin and splaying her small icy fingers flat against his chest in a way that sent his heart beating harder.

Dorrian swallowed, willing away his reaction to her. She was a frightened girl experiencing the worst, most terrifying day of her life. What she needed from him now was warmth and safety, nothing more.

If Evander had been there, he would have been able to rescue her long before she'd gotten quite this cold. Not to mention that he would have merely picked her up, his added heat as a dragon warming her up far more quickly than Dorrian could.

She spoke between violently chattering teeth. "You should leave. What if the dragon is still coming?"

"Don't worry about the dragon. He isn't coming." Dorrian couldn't help the wry note that crept into his voice at that. While things would have been a lot simpler for him if Evander had been there, he was strangely grateful that he was the one to go this time.

She released a long breath, her form slumping even more against him.

Her shivering turned into a different kind of shaking as sobs tore from her. She pressed her face into the folds of the blanket, sobbing hard enough she sounded ready to choke on the tears.

"You're safe now." Dorrian murmured the words into her hair, not sure if the girl could hear him over her

27

tears. "I'm so sorry for what you went through today. You're safe now. Nothing's going to happen to you."

He kept murmuring as he held her, letting her cry as she alternated between shaking and shivering, as if her body waffled between the fear and the cold.

After long minutes, she gave one last, gasping sob that ended in a long exhale. She sagged against him, as if utterly spent from all the tears and fear and cold.

Perhaps it was just as well Evander had never entrusted this duty to Dorrian before. Dorrian wasn't sure how Evander could stand it, seeing such stark fear over and over again. Dorrian would break if he had to witness such devastation mirrored in the eyes of another every few months.

Then again, perhaps Evander didn't have memories of horror of his own to shake through him, stealing his breath and coating his tongue with the remembered taste of blood and ash.

Maybe Dorrian hadn't experienced the same thing as this girl had, but he knew her fear, had tasted such terror.

Except in his case, there had been no one to rescue his family from the monsters, even if Evander had eventually rescued him from continued suffering at the hands of less than honorable dragons.

CLARISSA SNIFFLED her way to silence as painful tingles filled her slowly warming fingers and toes. She became aware of the stranger's strong arms around her, her head tucked beneath his chin against his chest. Her hands pressed against his chest, his shirt soft and warm against her fingers.

This was nice. Warm. Safe.

Except.

She was sitting on a stranger's lap. All but clinging to him.

Her face burned, and she struggled to lift her heavy head from his shoulder. "I should...this..."

"Shh. Wait until you're all the way warmed up." The stranger's arms tightened around her, though not constricting. She had the sense he wouldn't resist if she fought her way free of him.

Perhaps it was weak of her, but she slumped against him again, too weary and drained to want to argue. As long as she was held by this stranger, she didn't have to think about wolves or dragons or where she went from here.

They sat there in silence for several more minutes. Clarissa finally stopped shivering, though a bone cold ache still filled her.

"I'm Dorrian, by the way." The stranger's breath was a brief warmth against her hair before the cold mountain breeze swept it away.

She swallowed several times before she managed to croak out, "Clarissa."

"Well, Clarissa, I have some hot soup. I know you're probably not hungry, but it might help to warm you." The stranger—Dorrian—shifted her slightly, moving his arm so that her toes were no longer pinned between his arm and his body.

The draft of cold against her feet had her curling up tighter, tucking her feet up as she hugged her knees to her chest. Only after she'd resettled did she realize she'd rested her feet on top of his thigh.

This would be terribly embarrassing and highly improper, if she wasn't so cold and so beyond caring. Who was going to tell on her to the village elders? The dragon?

Not that there was anything romantic in this. This was just practical. And a tad uncomfortable, folded into a ball as she was.

Dorrian cleared his throat. "Uh, yes. The soup." He shifted again, reaching into what seemed to be a pocket near her feet. Yet a moment later, he withdrew a jug and a ceramic bowl that were both far too large to have been in a pocket.

With his arms still around her, he held the jug and the bowl out in front of the two of them, his cloak falling open and letting in more drafts of cold air.

Clarissa tugged the blankets around her more tightly. Perhaps the soup wouldn't be worth it, if she got cold in the process.

Unstoppering the jug, Dorrian poured some of the soup into the bowl. Then he swung the bowl carefully toward her.

Reluctantly, she wiggled her fingers out of the warmth of the blankets to grab the bowl. The ceramic was warm with the hot soup inside the bowl, and she cradled the bowl in both hands.

Dorrian stoppered the jug again and set it aside before he wrapped the cloak and his arms around her once again.

She blew on the soup, then took a tentative sip. The soup had a strange taste, but its warmth spread through her, helping to banish the chill that had settled into her bones.

Perhaps by the time she finished this soup, she'd be warm enough to reclaim her dignity, stop clinging to this stranger, and face whatever came next.

Chapter Three

By the time Clarissa finished her soup, Dorrian could tell by the way she was sitting up straighter, her eyes losing that haunted lack of focus, that she was returning to herself.

She took a final sip, then held up the bowl. "All done."

Dorrian gathered her in his arms again, then set her down beside him on the stone once again. The cold air rushed in to fill the space where she'd been, bringing with it a sense of loss.

He stood, stretching out stiff muscles. His legs had been well on their painful way to going to sleep while his rear end and the backs of his thighs were nearly numb from the freezing stone beneath him. How had she survived the hours she'd been tied there?

After retrieving the jug and bowl, Dorrian shoved them back into his pocket. Then he fished out the bundle of clothing Phoebe had given him. "As much as I wish I could heroically carry you all the way, I'm afraid I'm not quite that strong. We have a rather long walk ahead of us, and you'll want to bundle up."

The girl, Clarissa, reached for the clothing, her eyes wide and trusting when she looked up at him. "Where are we going?"

Dorrian hesitated. What should he tell her? Once he told her he was taking her back to the dragon, that trusting look would vanish, replaced with terror once more.

Perhaps it was wrong of him, but he rather liked the way she was looking at him now.

"Somewhere safe." To avoid her gaze, he took the stockings and boots, kneeling in the layer of snow before her. He worked the wool stockings over her small feet, before he tugged on the boots. They were a little big, but a good enough fit, especially with the thick stockings.

When he glanced up, he found Clarissa watching him, the blankets wrapped around her shoulders, her dark hair tumbling down her back.

He forced himself to drop his gaze, his throat clogging once again in that strange way. "Are you hurt at all? Did the ropes chafe your wrists?"

He hadn't gotten a good look at her wrists as he'd been freeing her, but Evander had mentioned the girls usually hurt themselves trying to escape the ropes.

Clarissa rubbed one of her wrists but shrugged. "They're fine."

Which meant they definitely weren't fine.

Dorrian pulled out the tin of balm and a roll of cloth

bandaging. "We might as well take a moment to tend them before we set out. Your wounds will chafe against the mittens otherwise."

Clarissa rubbed her wrist again, glancing at the forest around them, then at the nighttime sky. Then, with a sigh, she held out a hand to him.

Dorrian uncapped the balm, dipped in two of his fingers, then gently spread the balm over the abrasions circling her tiny wrist.

Once he'd spread the balm and bandaged her wrists, she pushed to her feet, sorting out the rest of the clothes he'd brought. With a glance at him, she tugged the wool dress over her head, putting it on over her other dress. He swiveled his gaze to the sky and didn't look down again until she said it was all right.

When she was bundled up in the hat, mittens, and scarf, Dorrian held out his hand. "I know this is going to be a strange request, but could you hold my hand? I don't want to get separated."

She glanced from his hand to his face. "How would we get separated?"

He might as well explain. They usually told the girls where they were as soon as possible, though he wasn't sure how she'd react if told this now, before she was safely in the castle. "Right now, we're in a faerie circle, a place where your Human Realm and the Greater Realm as you call it overlap, if you will. I'm going to be taking you deeper into the Greater Realm, and the boundary can be tricky for humans to navigate on their own unless they are a particularly skillful sort of human."

She stared at him for several heartbeats, her arms

hugged to her middle as if to wall away the night. "Greater Realm? Aren't...aren't you human?"

He wasn't sure how she'd react if he showed her his pointed ears, which were currently hidden beneath his knit cap. "I'm from the Greater Realm."

She edged back a step and bumped into the stone altar behind her. She reached a hand to steady herself as her legs buckled, though she managed to stay standing. "Then...then...I should..."

How much truth to tell her without scaring her more? Dorrian held his hands out, palms up, though his mittens made the gesture less effective than it normally would be. "I know it's frightening to cross the realms. But right now, the Greater Realm is the safest place for you. If you return to your village, the village elders won't let you stay. They might even kill you for not being a proper sacrifice for the dragon."

Her face washed white again, and this time she sat down, hard, on the stone. "I I can't leave, can I? I mustn't go with you. I need to wait for the dragon. He will be angry if he doesn't...if he isn't...and my village..."

She shook again, those violent shudders as her expression flattened into that numbed, terrified one once again.

Now he'd done it. He'd nearly had her feeling safe. And then he'd made the mistake of reminding her about the dragon and her purpose for being there.

He crossed the circle toward her again, kneeling at her feet so that he wasn't looming over her. "You don't have to worry about the dragon or your village. He won't hurt you, and he won't burn down your village."

A scrunch of confusion twisted her face along with the wide-eyed panic. "But...he's the dragon. He demands the sacrifices."

An ache filled him. If only he could tell her everything now and erase both that fear and confusion. But as much as his help so far this night had earned him a drop of her trust, it wouldn't be enough to overcome a lifetime of being taught otherwise by her parents and her village leaders.

He needed to be patient and tell her what he could in a way she would understand. Even if it meant that she would probably hate him, at least for a while, for what he was about to say next. Dorrian took her hand and met her gaze, savoring the last little bit of her trust before it was snuffed out. "I'm the dragon's steward. He sent me to take you to his castle."

For a long moment, she blinked at him. Then she yanked her hand out of his. "*You're* the dragon's steward. You...you were being so nice because...because...how can you be nice and work for the *dragon?*"

"Things aren't what they seem." Dorrian bit back a groan at his own words. Now he was using the same cryptic, non-answers that Evander gave the maidens. It always frustrated the poor girls to no end. He dragged in a breath, forcing himself to bare just a little bit of his heart. "I've seen monsters firsthand. There are dragons out there who do despicable things. But trust me when I say Evan—the dragon—isn't one of them."

Clarissa's hands curled into fists in her lap as she glanced away from him. "You're just saying that because you're the dragon's steward. You can't say anything bad about him."

"Oh, I certainly can. I'll tell you all about his flaws once we're safe and warm in the castle." Dorrian held out his hand once again. "Do you trust me enough to come with me?"

Clarissa glanced around the circle, as if taking in the dark evergreens and the even darker shadows beneath them. "No, not really. But I don't have much of a choice, now do I?"

"I'm sorry." Dorrian kept his hand stretched between them, waiting for her to make the move to take it. There wasn't much else he could say. He'd already done his best to reassure her, but she wouldn't fully believe him. Not until her own experiences at the castle challenged the beliefs her village had instilled in her.

With a sigh, Clarissa grasped his hand. Dorrian pulled her to her feet and led the way from the circle of evergreens, taking the thin track of a path that led upward into the mountain. He kept her hand clasped in his, trying to sense his way through the muddle that was the blurring of the realms. If he didn't get this just right, he'd find himself hiking to the top of the mountain in the Human Realm rather than toward Evander's castle in the Fae Realm.

After several long moments, Clarissa huffed, a burning edge to her voice. "You mean to tell me that I was sacrificed and nearly frozen to death or eaten by wolves, and the dragon couldn't even be bothered to fetch me himself?"

Dorrian could see how that would be a bit insulting, from her perspective. At least some of her fire was returning, if she was capable of being angry instead of tottering around in that shocked numbness from

37

earlier. "I would've thought you'd be happy to avoid the dragon."

"Yes. No." Her forehead scrunched as she heaved a gusty sigh. "I don't know. It just seems wrong that he wouldn't even show up after all of this." She flapped her hand, as if to indicate everything she'd been through that day.

Dorrian would've told her that the dragon would've been there if he could have, but he didn't think that would be reassuring to her.

He didn't have a chance to reply, for he'd found the edge of the overlapping realms. A swirling, upside-down feeling shivered over them, threatening to tug her away from him.

Then he stumbled through, pulling her with him, and the two of them stepped fully into the Fae Realm.

"What...what was that?" Clarissa trembled and huddled closer to him.

He probably shouldn't feel the thrill of pleasure that she was seeking safety with him. He was likely just the lesser of two scary things to her at the moment. "The boundary from the Human Realm into the Greater Realm. If you'd been with the dragon, the sensation wouldn't have been as strong, since dragons have an easier time moving between the realms than most."

She made a noncommittal sound in the back of her throat, as if she wasn't willing to admit anything positive about the dragon.

"We have a long walk ahead of us." Dorrian probably should have released her hand. It would have made walking easier for them.

He told himself it was because he didn't want her running off into the Fae Realm where he'd struggle to track her down before she was hurt. But that wasn't the whole truth. Or even most of it.

Chapter Four

Dorrian shuffled through the papers on the desk, but his heart wasn't in it this morning. All he could think of was the utter terror in Clarissa's eyes the night before. No matter what he said to reassure her—no matter how many times he'd told her the dragon wouldn't hurt her—she hadn't believed him. And once she'd learned he was the dragon's steward, what little trust she'd had in him as her rescuer had disappeared.

The door swung open, and Evander's measured tread strolled inside.

Dorrian glanced up, taking in the weary slump to Evander's shoulders. "How was dragon politics?"

"As frustrating and fiery as you might expect." Evander crossed his arms and leaned against the door jamb. "I heard the latest maiden was rescued last night."

"Yes." Dorrian shoved the paperwork around again without really seeing it. "I think we might have to handle this one differently. I'm the one who rescued her, so I'm the one she somewhat trusts."

"Are you sure you want to take this on?" Evander's amber-blue eyes searched Dorrian's face, though what he was looking to see written there, Dorrian couldn't guess.

Dorrian held Evander's gaze as steadily as he could. "Yes."

"All right. Just…be careful." Evander's gaze softened. "I know how the maidens remind you of yourself."

And there it was. Dorrian dropped his gaze back to the paperwork. What was he supposed to say to that? Yes, he had come face-to-face with real monsters, not to mention dragons who were less-than-honorable. Dorrian cleared his throat, still unable to meet Evander's gaze. "Perhaps. But I know just how fortunate they are that you are the dragon living in this mountain and not one of the others."

Evander heaved a long exhale. "I would rather they weren't sacrificed at all."

Dorrian agreed. But Evander had tried many times to stop the sacrifices in the early years. Dorrian hadn't been living here then, but he'd heard about the attempts. They hadn't gone well.

"Well, if you're going to take the lead, how do you want to handle this?" Evander gestured behind him in the general direction of the stairs and the maiden Clarissa.

"I think…you're the one who needs to go into hiding this time." Dorrian leaned back in the chair, finally able to look up again now that they were on a somewhat lighter topic.

Most of the time, Dorrian was relegated to the role of assistant steward while Evander played the part of steward. Rather badly, Dorrian might add, but the maidens didn't usually see the state of the study. But Evander wore authority too thickly on his broad shoulders to ever pass as the assistant.

As the assistant, Dorrian didn't interact with the maidens all that much. He was usually too busy keeping up with the paperwork.

Other times, Dorrian lived in the fae village for a few weeks, overseeing the work there, while the maiden was in residence.

"Entirely go into hiding. Got it." Evander sighed. "I'll have to sneak to the kitchens at night and stuff my pockets with food like a common thief."

"Don't be dramatic. Phoebe and I will bring you trays with plenty of food." Dorrian waved airily, trying to suppress his grin. The amount of food Evander consumed was a bit mind boggling, even knowing he was a dragon. He was pretty much always eating. "And none of your usual candle testing. I'll see if I can convince her to willingly speak with the dragon."

"That'll be trickier than you think it'll be. No matter how much you earn her trust, you're up against a lifetime of beliefs." Evander's words held the weight of decades of experience. "Deeply held beliefs aren't changed easily."

Perhaps it was hubris on Dorrian's part to think he could go about this in a different way than what Evander had developed over years of trial and error. Dorrian held Evander's gaze without flinching. "I know. I'll be mindful of that."

He would be. He didn't want to risk hurting Clarissa any more than she'd already been hurt by her own village.

CLARISSA PEEKED over the blanket as bright sunlight streamed around the curtains drawn over the window of her strange stone room in the mountain fortress.

After walking all night and into the morning, she'd barely glanced around before collapsing on the bed. Despite worries about the dragon, she'd still fallen asleep as soon as her head hit the pillow. At least the long walk had warmed her, and the cozy fire burning in the fireplace had banished the last of the cold.

What time of day was it? Should she get up? Even if she did, was she allowed to wander the fortress unescorted? Dorrian had pointed out some of the passageways as they'd come in that morning, but she'd been too tired to take in much.

A knock sounded on her door, and Clarissa clutched the blanket to her chin, as if a mere blanket would be enough if that was the dragon knocking on the door.

Would the dragon bother to knock? Or would he just burn the door down?

She swallowed several times before she could force her words out loud enough to be heard through the door. "Who is it?"

"Phoebe. We met briefly this morning." A woman's voice drifted from the passageway outside.

Clarissa released a breath and forced herself to sit up. "Come in."

A slightly plump woman with brown hair bustled inside, pushing a cart laden with dishes. "I brought you food. Not sure if you want to call it breakfast or supper at this time of day."

Clarissa's stomach rumbled, and she swung her legs off the bed. As she reached for the food, she halted. Was that bread...pink? And green eggs? What appeared to be a variety of fruit was various shades of magenta, fuchsia, and teal that she'd never seen from fruit before.

"Don't worry. It is all safe for you to eat." Phoebe handed her the plate with the pink bread. "I know the food here in the Fae Realm—Greater Realm—appears strange. But while you're under the dragon's protection, it will be safe to eat. I believe Dorrian explained that to you last night?"

"He did." Clarissa poked at the bread. She wasn't sure what to feel about Dorrian. He'd been kind last night, but he was also working for the dragon. He'd told her as much without even flinching.

How could he sound so proud about working for a monster like the dragon? He hadn't even batted an eye, even as he'd been taking her to the dragon for who-knew-what-purpose.

Would the dragon eat her once he returned? Was she, even now, being fattened up like a goat for slaughter in the fall?

And how could Dorrian smile at her and assure her that she'd be all right, all while knowing he was bringing her back to the dragon?

Clarissa choked down the toast, then nibbled at some of the fruit. The green eggs were a little too suspect-looking for her to dare eat.

Once she finished, she piled the plates back on the cart and wiped her hands on the napkin.

Phoebe bustled to the wardrobe and flung the doors open. "Looks like there's a good, sturdy dress in here for you. There aren't that many hours of daylight left, but you might as well get up, get dressed, and meet some of the others."

Others? What others?

A part of Clarissa wanted to stay in that room where it was safe—at least, as safe as anything was in the dragon's fortress.

"Has...has the dragon returned?" Clarissa dug her fingers into the blanket, the food she'd eaten churning in her stomach.

"Yes, this morning." Phoebe plucked the dress from the wardrobe and held it out to Clarissa. "But don't worry. You won't see him out and about during the day."

That was a small relief, at least. If Phoebe could be trusted. Phoebe, like Dorrian, worked for the dragon. Everything she said was suspect.

Clarissa took the dress, her fingers sinking into soft wool, as Phoebe reclaimed the cart.

Phoebe pushed the cart to the door, then halted in the doorway. "I'll be just outside when you're ready." The door snicked shut behind her.

Clarissa quickly dressed in the soft, red woolen dress. The boots were trimmed with white fur while the stockings were thick. She wouldn't get cold easily in this outfit.

As much as she wanted to linger, Clarissa forced her shoulders straight, faced the door, and forced her legs to move.

Outside in the passageway, Phoebe waited, the cart in front of her. She smiled, then led the way, the dishes on the cart rattling the whole time. They passed several doors and one branching tunnel before they reached a spacious room. A massive fireplace dominated one wall while a bank of windows was set into the far wall. Long tables with benches on either side filled the space. A kitchen nook opened on the far side from the fireplace, complete with another, smaller fireplace, cupboards, and a baking oven.

Dorrian leaned against the worktable in the kitchen area, inspecting the various plates of food laid out there.

"Don't you go raiding tonight's supper, now." Phoebe bustled ahead, industriously pushing the cart.

Dorrian snatched his hand away as if he feared a smack from a ladle. "You know I'd never do such a thing. That's more Evan…well, that's not normally my thing."

Phoebe rolled her eyes as she pushed the cart into a corner. "No, you're right. I've spent twenty-some years trying to fatten you up, and clearly it hasn't been working. I should be encouraging you to snatch as many treats as you like."

"Well, in that case…" Dorrian grinned and snagged one of the pastries. At least, Clarissa thought they were pastries. They were the right shape, even if they were the wrong color. He snagged a second one and held it out to Clarissa. "Are you full, or would you like one to take along for the tour?"

"Tour?" Clarissa had barely worked up the courage to follow Phoebe this far.

"Around the fortress. We came in so late last night—well, this morning—that there wasn't time to give you a proper tour." Dorrian strolled around the worktable to join her. He held out the pastry to her, as if she'd said yes to the food.

She took it. She wasn't that hungry, but nibbling on it would be something to do with both her mouth and her hands.

Dorrian ambled through the large room, and Clarissa glanced between him and Phoebe before she hurried to join him, the pastry crumbling and warm in her hand.

Why was Dorrian giving her a tour? A tour was something one gave a welcome guest, not a piece of meat being prepared for a dragon's meal.

Dorrian seemed to modulate his pace to match hers, munching on his pastry.

Clarissa crept along the corridor beside him, working up the courage to take a bite of her own pastry. When she finally took a nibble, the sweet taste melted on her tongue, the pink pastry filled with some kind of fuchsia-colored fruit jelly. "Hmm. This is good."

"Phoebe is quite a good cook. We are fortunate to have her." Dorrian smiled around a bite of pastry.

Clarissa just nodded and took another bite of the pastry. No words were needed for food this good.

DORRIAN SHOWED Clarissa around the main section of tunnels, from the central waterfall cavern to the tunnel that followed the creek to the room where most of the servants spent their days polishing stones. It wasn't work Dorrian would ever want to do long-term, but he could see the appeal of spending a day doing something mindless, chatting with the others, and keeping nice regular hours, something he rarely did as Evander's steward.

Clarissa turned all wide-eyed at her introduction to the gnomes. The three-feet-high gnomes took a bit of getting used to, especially the way they walked around with their hats pulled down to their noses, covering their eyes. If they had eyes. Dorrian wasn't entirely sure on that, since he'd certainly never seen them.

As they returned to the rock polishing room once again, Clarissa glanced around, rubbing her arms. "So… I'll be working in here? Polishing rocks?"

Dorrian opened his mouth, but the words stuck in his throat. He was supposed to tell her that she could polish rocks, if she wanted to. He was supposed to let her think that it was the dragon's purpose for her— anything to reassure her that the purpose wasn't to eat her.

Instead, what he found coming out of his mouth was, "No. Actually, you'll be working with me. I need an assistant."

He had no idea if she could read and write—some of the maidens could; others couldn't. If they could read and write in their own realm, the magic that translated speech worked on written words as well. But if they couldn't read or write in their own realm, they couldn't here either.

Clarissa's face blanched. "I wouldn't…I wouldn't

have to see the dragon, would I? I can't look upon his face."

"You don't have to see the dragon if you don't wish to see him." Dorrian reached a hand toward her but stopped short of actually touching her. If only there was something he could say that would reassure her. That didn't mean he wouldn't keep trying. "The dragon isn't as scary as your village made him out to be. He won't eat you."

He could see the moment she shut down. Her face stiffened, her dark brown eyes glazed, as she reasoned away his words with the twisted logic of her village elders. "Perhaps he will not eat me. But he will still burn my village and hurt my family if I don't do what he wants—whatever that is. Can you at least tell me that?"

She'd never believe him if he told her the dragon didn't want her for anything. He didn't have any grand purpose for demanding the maiden sacrifices...because he wasn't the one demanding them in the first place. The village elders were the ones who kept that superstition going all these years, despite Evander's best efforts to dissuade them.

"His purpose isn't what you think. But that will be for him to reveal once you wish to see him." Dorrian held the door open for her, waving for her to step into the tunnel with the creek winding through it. "But don't worry about that now. Come, I'll show you where I work."

Clarissa cast one last look at the rock polishers, lounging on various seats around the room, before she scurried through the doorway.

He led her back to the waterfall cavern, skirting

around the pool once again. He gestured to a tunnel with a grand staircase leading upward into darkness. "I work up there."

Clarissa eyed the stairs, cringing closer to Dorrian. "Is...is the dragon up there?"

Dorrian climbed the first couple of stairs, raising his voice and directing his words upward more than at her. "The dragon is not in the study. You won't see him at all."

There was a faint scuffling noise from the top of the stairs, then the click of the door. Dorrian caught a brief glimpse of Evander's boots as he all but threw himself across the landing and darted into the room across the way. That room held his hoard, and Evander wouldn't mind the excuse to spend time there.

Clarissa hovered at the base of the stairs, her gaze focused on the first step. "Are you...is it safe?"

"Perfectly safe, especially while you're with me." Dorrian held out his hand. Perhaps he shouldn't have added that last bit.

But when Clarissa rested her hand in his, his heart beat harder, his head light as if he might just float away. He clasped her cold, slim fingers with his, and it felt far more right than it should.

He climbed the stairs, going at her pace. She took the stairs one at a time, pausing on each stair as if she needed to gather her courage each time before proceeding to the next.

At the top, he turned her toward the door to the study, which was partially open. It must not have fully latched when Evander made his mad dash across the landing.

The door to Evander's hoard sanctuary was cracked open, and Evander peeked out, only one blue eye and a sliver of his form visible.

Dorrian made a shooing motion behind his back, mouthing to Evander over Clarissa's head, "Get back."

Evander smirked before he closed the door fully.

"This is the study." Dorrian pushed the door open and ushered Clarissa inside.

He had to bite his lip and suppress his indignation at the state of the room. The neat piles of paperwork Dorrian had left on the desk had somehow gotten strewn about while the morning's correspondence from the cubby was tossed carelessly on top. A few papers, letters, and scrolls had somehow ended up on the floor.

How had Evander managed to cause the study to be in such disarray in such a short amount of time? He'd just arrived back a few hours ago.

But that was Evander. Actually, dragons in general. They tended toward messiness when it came to paperwork.

Dorrian grabbed the nicer of the two chairs in the room and held it out for Clarissa. "I never asked. Can you read?"

She nodded as she took the seat. "Yes, though my handwriting isn't the most legible."

He didn't care what her handwriting looked like, as this was all just an excuse to spend time with her.

Purely to prove to her that the dragon wasn't to be feared. Nothing more.

Chapter Five

Clarissa resisted the urge to glance at Dorrian where he sat across the desk from her. She was supposed to be comparing the list of requested gemstones with the list of mined gemstones on hand and matching them up into a third allocation list to give to the gem polishers.

But after a month of helping Dorrian every day, it was getting harder and harder to resist that pull she felt around him. He was just so dedicated, studious, organized, and caring of those around them. Not to mention he was rather handsome on top of all that.

All that made it increasingly difficult to believe someone like Dorrian would work for a monster like a dragon.

Unless…he wasn't working for the dragon willingly. Was he, too, a captive of the dragon in some way?

She peeked up at him again. He was bent over another ledger, his dark hair falling over his swarthy skin and mussed around his tapered ears in a way that made her want to reach across the desk to smooth the strands.

As if feeling the weight of her gaze, Dorrian raised his head, his dark eyes meeting hers. "Was there something you needed?"

She cleared her throat, her mind buzzing in a way that left her tongue knotted. She found herself blurting, "The night you..." She wasn't sure what to call it. Rescued? Captured? "The night you took me from the stone, you mentioned something about being familiar with monsters. What did you mean by that?"

Dorrian froze, blinking at her over the stacks of papers and ledgers on the desk between them. Then he deliberately set down his pen and leaned back in his chair. "It's a long, rather painful story. Are you sure you want to hear it?"

Did she? She had a feeling it was the type of story that was going to make her heart ache with compassion for the fae sitting across from her, sending her dangerously deeper towards falling in love with him.

But there was so much she didn't understand. So much that didn't add up. She'd spent a month in this fortress without seeing hide nor scale of the dragon. He hadn't demanded anything of her, despite his demand for a maiden sacrifice. Every person in this fortress was unfailingly loyal to the dragon. At first, she'd thought it fear.

But the only one afraid in this fortress was her. That shouldn't be the case if the dragon was as terrible as the village elders made him out to be.

She needed to understand, and if this story was the

way to go about it, then she would listen, despite the danger to her heart.

"Yes, I'd like to hear it." She set down her own pen, rolling the stiffness out of her shoulders.

Dorrian released a long breath, his gaze lowering from hers as he rolled his pen over the ledger with a finger. "I was born in the Court of Sand, one of the fae summer courts. The barriers that separate the courts from both the Human Realm and the Realm of Monsters are particularly thin in that court's deserts. The realms bleed into each other, and the Court of Sand is always getting attacked by creatures from the Realm of Monsters. Phoenixes, fiery foxes, lightning birds, and sand dragons—a lesser dragon that isn't intelligent like the Greater Dragons—are a constant threat."

"It sounds dangerous." Clarissa clasped her hands in her lap to avoid reaching for his hand.

"It is." Dorrian's voice roughened. "When I was very little, the monsters were so bad that they were driving people from their homes, including my village and my family. We had to flee, living in roving camps trying to escape the monsters. But it wasn't enough. My parents and my siblings…they…" Dorrian's tone dropped lower, his gaze still avoiding hers. "I watched the monsters kill them."

"I'm so sorry." Clarissa couldn't help it. She reached across the desk and rested a hand over his. "That's so awful. How old were you?"

"Six." Dorrian didn't look at her, nor did he seem to react to her touch. But he didn't pull his hand away, so perhaps a non-reaction was something after all. "The rulers of the court were so desperate that they made a bargain with several flights of dragons for protection. Except that they then broke the bargain, and the dragons turned on them. In their fury, the dragons raided the Court of Sand, carrying many people off as their due for aiding the court. Including me."

"That's how you ended up bound to the dragon." Clarissa shivered, trying not to imagine a tiny, six-year-old Dorrian being carried away in the claws of a dragon.

"Yes. And no." Dorrian finally lifted his head, a faint smile creasing his mouth, though it didn't yet reach his eyes. "I would have been bound to a dragon, a captive turned slave until the binding could be broken, if not for one particular dragon. Our dragon. He rescued me, broke the binding on me, and gave me a home. I've served him willingly and freely ever since."

Huh. That was not the answer to the story she'd been expecting. Unless Dorrian only thought he was serving willingly and freely but he really wasn't? Wasn't there a phenomenon where captives came to care for their captors after a while? A defense mechanism of the psyche? How would she be able to tell if that were the situation in this case?

Dorrian sighed, the smile fading. "I can see you don't believe me. I know why you don't, but I wish you'd trust me when I say I've been a captive of dishonorable dragons before. This dragon isn't one of them."

If only she could believe him. He looked so sincere, looking at her with his deep brown eyes set in that slim, fae face, his slightly long black hair sweeping across his forehead in a way that made her fingers itch to brush it out of his eyes.

She found herself leaning forward, pulled in by the vulnerable look to his eyes, the open and all-too-trustworthy expression across his face. When she finally managed to speak, her voice coming out in little more than a whisper, all that came out was, "I'm sorry about your family. I don't know the loss of death, but I've lost my family too."

Talking about the loss of family was better than dwelling on the dragon. At least that topic was merely painful, not fraught with pretty lies spoken oh so sincerely.

He blinked, and the moment broke. He leaned against the back of his chair once again, that vulnerable expression shuttering into something kind, pleasant, but still hiding the depths she'd briefly glimpsed. "I should have told you before. I've mucked this all up. Clarissa, you're free to visit your family, if you'd like. They'll find it a shock that you've returned from the dead, and we'll have to be careful on how we sneak in and out of Thysia because we can't let anyone else see you."

Clarissa gripped the edge of the desk, her head whirling. It had never even occurred to her to ask to visit. She was the sacrifice. She was supposed to be dead. In a way, she had been living like she was dead to her family, forbidden to ever return.

Was Dorrian lying about this? Surely he wouldn't toy with her. Not about this. Not after what had happened to his own family.

"Could I...really?" She couldn't get more than the incoherent words to croak out of her throat.

"Yes, of course. It's too late in the day to set out now,

but I can make the arrangements and we can set out first thing in the morning, if you'd like." Dorrian gestured toward the window. "It will be a long hike both there and back, and I hope you don't mind if I come along as escort and protection from the fae monsters that roam the forest."

She shuddered at the memory of both the wolves that had come close to eating her and that long, cold hike up the mountain afterwards. "I'll be glad of the company. Thank you for taking the time from your duties to provide an escort."

"I'm happy to do it." Dorrian flashed her a smile, one that lit his eyes and sent a flutter through her stomach.

Was it wrong the way her heart beat harder? She should be focused on the joy of seeing her family again. That was there, but it was hard to believe it could be real.

But more than that was the anticipation of a long walk with just Dorrian. Yes, she spent every day, nearly all day, with Dorrian as it was. But they were working, and much of their talk was of work.

A long stroll like that would be almost romantic.

She shoved that thought aside and cleared her throat. "Will the dragon let you—let both of us—go for that long?"

"He won't mind." Dorrian's answer was quick. Easy. As if he knew the dragon so well he didn't have to think about it. As if the dragon was more a friend than his lord.

A sign that the dragon was a good dragon, as he'd said? Or a sign that Dorrian was deeply blinded by his long captivity?

Either way, she wouldn't question it. Even if this was a trick, what did she have to lose at this point? The dragon hadn't even bothered to show his face—not that she was even allowed to see his face—ever since she'd arrived. There was something so very wrong about that. It was almost as if the dragon didn't even want her.

Which made no sense, given that he was the one to demand the sacrifices in the first place. What dragon demanded a sacrifice, then didn't even do anything with the sacrifice?

Perhaps her walk with Dorrian, the time away from this fortress, and, most of all, her visit with her family would give her some clarity about the dragon and this strange situation she found herself in.

Maybe, if she was very fortunate, she would figure out what she felt for Dorrian while she was at it.

DORRIAN STRODE ALONG THE PATH, heading downward from the mountain castle, Clarissa trotting along at his side. His pockets were so stuffed with camping supplies, food, and weapons that the pockets felt heavy, despite the magic.

He risked a glance upward, but he couldn't spot Evander, who had volunteered to shadow them on their walk to make sure they didn't run into any trouble. Dorrian could handle a sword well enough that he wouldn't accidentally stab his own foot, and he had scared off those wolves. But anything more monstrous than that would be more than Dorrian could handle.

Evander's mere presence would keep the monsters from even coming close enough to trouble them.

Dorrian let the silence linger for a while as they walked, just enjoying the comfortable companionship of Clarissa's presence.

Would she mind if he held out his arm? Or, better yet, took her hand?

He shouldn't. She was a captive. By the laws of the Fae Realm, *his* captive, even if she believed herself the captive of the dragon. There was so much she didn't understand because she couldn't see the truth just yet, and until she did, he couldn't free her the way Evander had him so many years ago.

It would be beyond dishonorable to let anything develop between them in such circumstances, no matter how he loved the way she laughed, the way her eyes lit with her smiles, the look of a pen in her hand as she bent over one of the ledgers. Wrong as it was, his heart tugged to her whenever she stepped into a room, making him dream of family in a way he hadn't dared for years.

Speaking of family...he didn't want to bring this up. Didn't want to remind himself of his blunder, even if Evander had assured him that, based on his limited observations, Clarissa wouldn't have been ready for the trip back to her family before now.

But Clarissa needed to know, before she was as shocked as her family would be when she saw them.

"Clarissa, there's something you ought to know before we make the crossing into the Human Realm." Dorrian risked a glance at her. She had tipped her face to the sky, a smile lingering.

But at his words, the smile dropped as she glanced at him. "Is something wrong? Something to do with the dragon?"

"Yes. No." Dorrian sighed. "Nothing to do with the dragon. It's about the differences between the realms. Time doesn't move the same way between the Human Realm and the Greater Realm. While a month has passed here, more time will have passed there. Several months, most likely."

He forced himself to watch her face whiten under the realization that her family had believed her dead for months.

He should have brought up a trip back sooner, even if she hadn't been ready to hear it.

But this was the pain of the abominable sacrifices. Even if he or Evander went to the village and told her family she was alive, her family likely wouldn't believe them. Even if they brought a note in her handwriting, it would only be a shock her family would discard in disbelief. They would only believe seeing Clarissa alive and well with their own eyes, and even that would be harder than Clarissa realized.

"My family has thought me dead for months?" Clarissa's steps stuttered, her eyes wide in her pale face.

"I'm afraid so." Dorrian halted, turning to her. At the wobble to her knees, he reached out a hand, gently grasping her elbow to steady her. "It will be a shock to them to see you return. Between their fear of the dragon and the shock, they might not react the way you expect when you see them."

Clarissa sucked in a long breath before she nodded.

But she didn't pull away from his grasp, and it was left to him to finally drop his hand.

They set out again, and this time the silence wasn't as comfortable, too filled with his revelations and her pain. It almost made him wish he'd kept his mouth shut until they were closer to her home.

The sun beamed warm this morning, or as warm as the sun ever was in the fae winter courts. Snow piled alongside the path and layered over the branches of the spruces on either side. The thin layer of fresh snow frosting the path crunched under their boots. With the good weather, birds flitted among the trees, warbling out their songs. None of them appeared to be the dangerous kind of bird or a tricky pixie in disguise of which he'd need to be wary.

At least the walk down the mountain was far easier than the trek up, even if the front of his legs began to burn after a while from holding himself back against the slope.

After several hours of walking, Dorrian found a large rock next to the trail, its surface so warmed by the sun that all the snow had melted and the rock's surface was dry.

Dorrian halted and gestured to the rock. "Let's rest for a moment."

Clarissa sank onto the rock, massaging her legs through her thick skirt. "I thought I was in good shape, but I'm not used to hiking up and down mountains."

"Me neither." Dorrian perched at the very end of the rock. He was still far too close, his shoulder and arm brushing against her.

But the rock was the only dry place to sit, and he didn't exactly mind sitting so close to her.

She didn't appear to mind either. She didn't stiffen or try to pull away from him. If anything, she shifted slightly closer, though perhaps she was merely trying to find a comfortable spot on the rather lumpy and hard rock.

It was a good thing Evander usually flew this route high in the sky, otherwise he might have snatched away this rock to add it to his hoard. Though, Evander usually tried to confine his rock hoarding to smaller rocks. If he collected boulders, he'd fill up the mountain in no time. As much as Dorrian teased Evander about his dragon tendency toward hoarding—and general messiness—to his credit, he tried to go about hoarding in the healthiest way possible.

"Would you like a snack while we rest?" Dorrian reached into his pocket and rummaged around for a moment. Even with the magic, the pocket was so stuffed that it took a second or two for the basket of food he was looking for to come to hand.

As he pulled it out, Clarissa blinked and shook her head, a faint smile breaking through the reverie she'd fallen into during their walk. "Even after a month, I'm still not used to these magical pockets. It is so strange that you can just pull a whole basket out of a pocket as if it is nothing."

"So strange that you humans only have regular pockets that don't hold much." Dorrian grinned back as he set the basket on his knees. He opened the top, inspecting the generous portions of food Phoebe had stuffed inside. "What would you like? Looks like there is everything from sandwiches to fruit pastries to a variety of other desserts. It appears Phoebe wanted to make sure we not only didn't starve, but we also didn't feel so much as a pinch of hunger."

Clarissa laughed, then reached past him to pull out a fruit pastry. "I'm rather fond of these. I hope Phoebe packed plenty."

"Looks like she did." Dorrian picked one for himself, closed the basket, then stuffed it back into his pocket. He leaned closer to Clarissa, dropping his voice. "And if she didn't, I raided the kitchens early this morning, and I have a second basket with more desserts in my pocket in case this basket runs out."

"You didn't." Clarissa laughed, then lightly shoved him. "There won't be anything left for everyone else back at the castle."

"Phoebe will give me a scolding when we get back, but it will have been worth it." Dorrian took a huge bite of his pastry, the sweetness bursting across his tongue. "Besides, she'll whip something up and enjoy having the excuse to do a little more baking."

Clarissa shared a smile and bit into her own fruit pastry.

Once they both finished their pastries, they set out once again.

Dorrian let the silence stretch into the comfortable rhythm of walking before he dared to ask, "What is your family like?"

Clarissa's face blanched again, and something in her stilled into wariness again. "Are you asking for yourself or for the dragon?"

Dorrian's heart pinched once again. The rumor went

around the village that the dragon made the families of the sacrificed maidens disappear. That was partly true, but the disappearance was voluntary as the families moved to be with their daughters once they, too, saw the truth about the village leaders and the dragon.

But Clarissa wasn't quite ready to see that yet. Perhaps soon. Tonight might be rather shattering for Clarissa.

Dorrian held Clarissa's gaze. "I'm asking for myself. I won't tell any of what you share to the dragon."

An easy promise to make. Evander wouldn't press.

Besides, Dorrian *was* asking for himself. He wanted to know Clarissa better. Her family. Her thoughts. Her dreams.

Clarissa's shoulders gave a little shudder as she looked away. But the color returned to her face as she released a breath, her stride more relaxed once again. "I see. In that case…"

She began to talk about her family. Her parents ran one of the many small olive presses that filled Thysia. She had several younger sisters, but no brothers, which put the inheritance of her family's holdings in question, depending on the sons-in-law her sisters brought into the family someday.

As she talked, her face lit up, a bounce to her stride that Dorrian hadn't seen the whole time she'd been on the mountain.

It shouldn't have been like this. The sacrifices ripped young women from their homes, put them through a terrifying experience, and all for no purpose whatsoever besides the village elders maintaining control over Thysia.

Yet was it wrong that a tiny piece of him was slightly grateful for the sacrifices? He never would have met Clarissa if not for them. Not that he could ever act on the feelings that had been growing inside his heart.

Not that he didn't think the sacrifices were utterly wrong and should be ended as soon as possible. But he wasn't going to overlook a very pretty, very diligent, very intelligent silver lining either.

Chapter Six

Clarissa sobbed as she stumbled almost blindly around the corner of the house, all but falling into Dorrian's arms where he stood in the shadows of an alley between houses on the outskirts of Thysia.

Her reunion with her family had been going so well. They'd been shocked to see her alive, but joyous.

Then she'd mentioned the dragon. And everything had fallen apart.

She'd made the mistake of saying she hadn't even spoken with the dragon or been in his presence.

Her parents had been so afraid that the dragon was displeased in some way. More, they had feared what the village elders might do if they discovered she had returned without doing whatever she was supposed to do to appease the dragon.

The next thing she knew, she was being cast out and told to hurry back to the dragon as quickly as she could.

None of this made sense. Was the dragon displeased? Was that why he'd been avoiding her?

And yet he hadn't burned the village. He hadn't hurt her. Dorrian, his steward, had repeatedly reassured her that she was safe, and the dragon wasn't angry.

Who was she to believe? Her parents and village elders whom she'd known all her life? Or the dragon's steward she'd known only a month?

Why was her heart telling her to listen to the latter?

Dorrian held her, his hand tracing a gentle line up and down her back. "Shh. It's all right."

It wasn't. Far from it. But when he was holding her like this, she could almost believe him.

Lights flared on in the house near her parents', voices rising from inside.

Dorrian's hand stilled on her back, his grip around her going tighter. "Looks like we woke the neighbors. It's all right to cry, but maybe wait until after we're safely out of here."

Clarissa gulped back the tears, stuffing them away as best she could. She swiped a sleeve over her face and nodded.

Dorrian released her but only long enough to take her hand and tug her deeper into the alley.

They wound their way through the outskirts of Thysia until they were once again surrounded by the groves of olive trees for which the village was famous.

Clarissa glanced in the direction of the track that would take her toward her friend Nessa's home. She longed to let Nessa know that she was alive.

But what would she say? What if Nessa and her

parents acted the same way Clarissa's parents had? She wasn't sure she could bear a second confrontation that night.

Dorrian slowed his steps to match her hesitating pace, glancing over his shoulder. "Was there someone else you wished to see?"

"My friend Nessa. She's like a sister to me." Clarissa paused, torn, even as more lamps flared to life in the village behind them. She didn't think her parents would breathe a word of her visit, but had the neighbors seen or heard anything? "But…"

"We should keep moving." Dorrian provided the excuse. "The village elders might punish you—even kill you—if they believe you haven't done your part as the village sacrifice."

That possibility was all too real, too true. Those same village elders had been willing to sacrifice her to a dragon, believing she was going to be horrifically eaten. There was no telling what else they'd do to her in the name of the sacrifices.

Perhaps it was the coward's way out, but Clarissa nodded and set out on the path toward the mountain once again, turning her back on Nessa and the rest of Thysia.

DORRIAN LEFT CLARISSA to her thoughts as they hiked up the mountain again. The evergreen circle with its stone slab in the center was the best way to get back into the Fae Realm—for him, anyway. Evander would've had a much easier time.

Clarissa shivered as they passed the stone, walking closer to him and keeping her eyes averted from the place where she'd nearly died. He couldn't help his own shiver, remembering how the wolves had been gathering around her.

Taking her hand, he plunged between the evergreens, the whirl of realms meeting churning around them, until they finally stumbled out the other side.

The moon shone high in the sky, bathing the snow on the branches of the evergreens in silver.

For the first time since leaving Thysia, a spark returned to Clarissa's gaze as she looked around. "It is still night here. I thought you said time moves differently between the Greater Realm and the Human Realm."

"It does." Dorrian shrugged, scanning the forest ahead of them. "But when crossing the barrier between them, it does have a tendency to match up night-to-night and day to day, even if the time passing between the realms isn't matched. I don't really understand it either."

Clarissa made a murmur of acknowledgement, her steps slowing as she trudged through the deep snow.

Dorrian searched the path ahead until he finally spotted what he'd been looking for. A thin track branched away from the main trail. He gestured to it. "There's a camping spot off the trail just ahead. We'll camp there for the rest of the night before hiking back to the castle in the morning."

Clarissa nodded again, already panting at the incline. After the events in Thysia, her weariness was probably hitting her hard. They'd been hiking since that morning with very few rests. If they tried to hike back to the castle that night, they'd be up for a full day and a full night.

At least they'd be safe camping here. Even if the villagers had seen something and woken the village elders, anyone following them up the mountain would struggle to get through the barrier between the realms, mere humans as they were.

He tramped down the track and soon found a small clearing, sheltered by tall pines. The clearing was almost suspiciously clear of snow, the ground completely dry, while a fireplace had been formed of stones in the center of the space. The fireplace had openings in three of its sides with a short stack of a chimney rising over the center.

"We'll set up camp here." Dorrian dug into his pockets and began unloading the equipment. "Do you know how to set up a tent?"

Clarissa shook her head, swaying a bit on her feet.

"Not a problem." Dorrian formed two piles of supplies. Then he set to work, directing Clarissa on where she could help.

Between the two of them, they soon had the two canvas tents set up on either side of the fireplace with the openings ready to pour warmth into each tent.

While Clarissa busied herself in her tent, setting up the bearskin rug, bedroll, and blankets he'd given her, Dorrian tromped deeper into the forest, following a set of footprints that led away from the clearing.

When he was out of sight of the clearing, he called, keeping his voice soft, "Evander?"

"Here." Evander's deep voice rumbled from somewhere to Dorrian's left.

Dorrian turned in that direction, finding Evander crouched in the shadows of a sweeping spruce tree, picking up another fallen branch to add to the pile he had in his arms. He was dressed only in a light tunic and breeches stuffed into tall boots, utterly impervious to the cold, thanks to being a dragon.

His wings were folded as tightly as they could be against his back. While being in half-dragon form was more ungainly for Evander in this forest, he was better able to defend against monsters in this form. Perhaps not as well as he could once he shifted into a full dragon, but this form wouldn't frighten Clarissa so much if she should catch sight of him.

Evander rose, and his wings knocked into the spruce tree. Clumps of snow fell onto Evander's head and shoulders. He scowled up at the spruce tree before he headed in Dorrian's direction, his footsteps crunching loudly on the snow. When he spoke, his tone was a gravelly whisper. "How was her visit?"

"As bad as you warned me it would be." Dorrian stuffed down the ache of the memory of Clarissa's tears. "I think she might be ready to meet the dragon. If I were to guess, she spent our whole walk back here questioning everything she's ever been told about the dragon."

Evander nodded, then he held out the stack of logs and sticks in his arms. "You'd better get back before she decides to look for you."

Dorrian held his arms out, grunting as Evander shifted the pile onto his arms. The pile was unexpectedly heavy. Evander had made it look so easy. But then again, he was a dragon.

Evander smirked as he stepped back. "Not too heavy?"

"Nope. Not at all." Dorrian's voice held a strained note. One of the sticks was digging a nob of a broken branch into his forearm while his biceps strained under the unaccustomed weight. But he wasn't about to admit out loud how heavy it was.

Spinning on a heel, Dorrian tottered back the way he'd come. With the pile of logs and sticks in his arms, he had to walk upright, unable to duck under the branches as he had on the way there. He got a few face-fuls of pine needles and snow before he popped out into the clearing once again.

Clarissa crawled out of her tent. "I was just wondering where you had gone."

"Just collecting firewood." Dorrian dropped the pile next to his tent, trying to muffle his sigh of relief. No way he'd admit how much his arms were trembling by the end.

Kneeling in front of the fireplace, Dorrian broke one of the sticks into small pieces of kindling, sticking them inside. He piled larger logs over them, then stuffed several of the crannies with dry grasses.

While he worked, Clarissa rolled one of the two rather conveniently dry logs to a spot next to the fire-place between their two tents before she perched on it.

Once he had the wood prepared, Dorrian dug into his pocket and pulled out a stone jar with a hinged, stone lid. Carefully, he held the jar toward his prepared firewood, then pulled open the lid with his other hand.

A tongue of blue flame licked above the rim of the jar. He held it to one of the packs of dried grasses. When it caught, he moved on to another spot until he had several places alight and burning merrily. He capped the stone jar, then deposited it in his pocket once again.

As he rose, his feet tingling from crouching for so long, he glanced at Clarissa.

Her eyes were wide as she glanced from his magical pocket to the fire. "What was that?"

"Stored dragon fire." Dorrian kept his tone casual as he rolled the second log closer and sat down so close his shoulder nearly brushed hers. "What's the point of keeping a dragon around if you have to light fires the hard way?"

Something rustled at the edge of the clearing, but Dorrian pointedly ignored whatever—well, whoever —it was.

Instead, he dug into his now much emptier pockets and withdrew the basket of food again. "I don't know about you, but I've worked up quite the appetite with all our walking."

He held out one of the cold sandwiches to Clarissa, and she took it, eating in an almost defeated silence for several minutes.

He had finished one sandwich and was working on his second by the time Clarissa drew in a deeper breath, her shoulders shuddering as if shaking beneath the weighty matters she'd been pondering on their hike.

When she turned to him, her dark brown eyes searched his face. "Why does the dragon demand sacrifices?"

It was time for the truth, if she'd hear it. Dorrian

held her gaze, hoping beyond hope that his words would sink in rather than be rejected. "He doesn't. He never has. In fact, he has done his best to end the sacrifices."

"Then why..." Clarissa gestured at herself, as if unable to ask what she was even doing there if the dragon didn't actually want sacrifices.

"It's a long story, one that would be better coming from him." Dorrian glanced over his shoulder, catching sight of Evander, who was doing a bad job of hiding himself behind a tree. His wings were far too bulky to hide. "I have a confession to make. The dragon has been providing an escort for us today, staying out of sight while he makes sure no true fae monsters attack us on our walk."

Clarissa's spine stiffened, her eyes widening. "He's... he's here now?"

"Yes. Who do you think made sure our campsite was dry and the fire easy to light?" Dorrian held out his hand to her, though he didn't presume to take her fingers in his. "You can meet him, if you're ready. You don't have to fear him. He's not going to hurt you. He isn't going to fly into a rage if you see his face. After all, I look at his ugly mug all the time. It's nothing special."

Out of the corner of his eye, Evander let his head sag back, as if searching the sky for patience when dealing with impertinent stewards.

Dorrian's humor didn't seem to ease much of Clarissa's fear. She shivered, staring down at his hand for several long minutes.

Then she clasped his hand, squeezing so tightly his

fingers ached. But he didn't pull away. His heart beat harder at this sign of her trust in him.

"Do you promise?" Clarissa squeezed her eyes shut, her knuckles white as she clutched his hand. "Do you promise that the dragon won't hurt me and won't hurt anyone in my village?"

The tips of his fingers were going red from her squeezing, but he didn't pull away. "I promise. The dragon won't hurt you. He won't hurt anyone in your village. He won't burn so much as a single olive tree. Unless he sneezes and does it by accident."

Perhaps the joke had been in poor taste because Clarissa paled instead of laughing. At least Dorrian got a silent eyeroll and scowl out of Evander.

Dorrian rested his free hand over their clasped ones. "I promise. I'll be right here the whole time."

Clarissa let out another shuddering breath, then gave a stiff nod. "All right. I'd like to meet the dragon. I need answers."

"I'll be happy to provide your answers." Evander's voice came from behind them, low and slightly growling in his half-dragon form.

Clarissa squeaked and somehow managed to squeeze Dorrian's fingers even tighter.

Dorrian patted their clasped hands with his free hand. At least he'd given her his right hand to clutch. He might end up with broken fingers before this night was over, and he'd need his left hand—his dominant hand— in working order. "Clarissa, this is Evander. The dragon."

She trembled, much as he had as a boy, facing the

monsters of his childhood who'd snatched his family away.

Forget trying to preserve his fingers. He took her other clenched fist in his own, cradling both her hands. "Clarissa, do you trust me? I'm right here. You can open your eyes. Nothing is going to happen to you."

He wished he could take this fear away. If only he could reassure her that she was safe.

But he would be patient, much as Evander and Phoebe had been for him in those early years.

CLARISSA SUCKED IN A DEEP BREATH, stilling, her heart hammering painfully hard in her chest and roaring in her ears.

If she was wrong about Dorrian, if this was all some twisted trick, then she was going to die in the next few minutes.

But if she was right…if Dorrian was as trustworthy as his grip on her hands suggested, then her whole concept of the world was about to shatter still further.

Slowly, she peeled her eyes open, taking in Dorrian sitting across from her, his dark brown eyes focused on her face. With the last of her courage, she raised her head and looked in the direction the deeper voice had come from.

A man stood there, dressed in a light blue tunic that did little to hide the breadth of his shoulders. A pair of dark blue, leathery wings rose from his back, silhouetted against the moonlight. The light of the fire cast shadows across his chiseled jaw and danced in his eyes.

He was the dragon, and she had just looked at his face.

She flinched and slammed her eyes shut again. Was this it? Was she going to die?

She waited one heartbeat. Two. Three.

Nothing happened.

Drawing in another deep breath, Clarissa cracked one eye open and peeked at the dragon again. "You aren't angry that I looked at your face, are you?'

"No." The dragon—Evander, as Dorrian had called him—held his hands toward her, palms up. "I suppose that according to the village elders, I'm the kind of unstable, vainglorious dragon who flies into a rage if anyone dares look upon me, but I'm not what your village has made me out to be."

Nothing had been like the village elders said it would be from the moment she'd been left on that stone.

It was time to let herself think that the village elders were wrong. Perhaps she couldn't fully wrap her mind around it, but she would trust the man—fae—holding her hands and telling her that everything would be all right if she faced whatever this truth might be.

Clarissa fully opened her eyes, this time forcing herself to gaze at the dragon without looking away. "You look surprisingly...normal."

Except for the wings and an angular shape to his face, he didn't look all that different than all the other fae she'd seen at the mountain fortress. Taller and broader than Dorrian, but not what she had been expecting. Not that she was even sure what her expectations had been.

"I can shift into a full dragon, but this half-dragon form fits in the clearing better." He spoke oddly, as if he was trying not to move his lips too much. "I can also shift into a form that appears like a normal fae. Do you mind if I shift into that? I keep knocking snow off the branches with my wings."

"Awkward things, wings." Dorrian leaned closer to her, lowering his voice conspiratorially, though he still spoke loudly enough that the dragon would probably hear. "Notice how he's trying to hide his itty-bitty fangs."

"They are not itty-bitty." The dragon spoke between lips nearly mashed together so that not a hint of teeth showed while he talked.

"They are compared to your full-sized dragon fangs." Dorrian smirked, his eyes twinkling in the firelight.

There was something about the banter. Dorrian had no fear of teasing the dragon, as if he was utterly unafraid that Evander would shift into a full dragon and gobble him up or burn him to a crisp for the insults.

More than that, Dorrian was relaxed and laughing in a way that was...brotherly. That was the sense she was getting, watching the dragon and his steward. She'd wondered if Dorrian was just loyal to the dragon because he'd been bound so long that he didn't even realize how much of a captive he was.

But that wasn't the case. Far from it. Dorrian and Evander were as close as brothers, bonded by long years of friendship.

And that unsettled every conception of the dragon she'd had, even more than seeing him in person.

Dorrian could never have been brothers with the dragon portrayed by her village elders.

But the dragon Dorrian had been telling her about? The one who wouldn't hurt her, who had never wanted sacrifices, and who was kind enough to rescue a scared little boy from the dishonorable dragons—now that dragon was one Dorrian would claim as a brother.

"Shouldn't you be older?" Clarissa gestured from Dorrian to Evander. "Dorrian said you saved him from the other dragons when he was a boy. But you look the same age, more or less."

Before her eyes, something about the dragon blurred, his wings shrinking, his face going indistinct. Then he was standing before her, wingless, his face less reptilian and more human. Well, fae, given his pointed ears. If she'd run into him on the path, she never would have guessed he was a dragon and wasn't just a normal fae like Dorrian.

Evander shrugged his broad shoulders. "I am a Greater Dragon. I don't age as quickly as other fae."

Huh. This probably shouldn't be the question she should be dwelling on, but it was somehow easier to focus on Dorrian and Evander rather than on the dragon and her village.

Evander reached into a pocket, pulled out a folding stool, popped it open, and sat down, leaving several feet between her and him, as if he didn't want to crowd her. He regarded her with eyes that appeared some kind of blue in the flickering firelight. "Are you ready for answers?"

She nodded, though her world was tilting so much already she wasn't sure what she'd do if it tilted further.

The only thing keeping her steady was Dorrian's grip on her hands and the steady way he was looking at her.

Perhaps now that the dragon no longer lurked between them, this *something* stretching between them could grow into more.

Chapter Seven

Clarissa strolled hand-in-hand with Dorrian as they navigated the path from the mountain fortress—eyrie, as Evander called it—to the fae village nestled in the valley at the base of the mountain.

The past week had been one of tearing down and rebuilding in her mind as she examined everything she'd been told was the truth and held it up to the light of the real truths.

But at the end of it, she found herself stronger, freer, and more at peace than she had ever been in her life before.

If only she could figure out where she went from here.

The fae village turned out to be quaint, despite the strange people strolling about. In among the fae were a few of the other formerly sacrificed maidens and their families who had moved here. Many of the girls had families of their own now.

Clarissa paused in front of one of the small but neat cottages that lined one of the side streets. She hugged her arms over her stomach, trying to hold in the ache in her heart. "Before all this happened, all I wanted was to settle down with a good man and raise a family. I thought I'd find someone who could take over the olive press from my father someday."

"Clarissa, that can still happen." Dorrian reached for her, then dropped his hand. "It might look different than what you imagined, but you can still have that home and that family." He gestured at the row of cottages. "Several of these are empty, just waiting to be claimed."

She glanced from him to the adorable cottage before her. Just the kind of home she had pictured for herself. Perhaps a bit more snow piled on the roof than the one she'd dreamed about as a child, but her dreams could shift and grow, as could she.

Her heart in her throat, she gathered her courage, though she couldn't look at Dorrian. "That dream would be rather incomplete without a good man to share it with."

A bit forward of her, yes. But she didn't want Dorrian to mistake her meaning.

This time when he reached for her, he didn't withdraw. Instead, he took her hand, tugging her closer. "What about a fae?"

"As I'm going to be spending the rest of my life in the Fae Realm, a fae would make the most sense." Clarissa peeked up at Dorrian, finally meeting his gaze.

His deep chocolate-brown eyes held her gaze. He lifted his hand and cradled her cheek. "And if I'm the dragon's steward? You'll never be fully free of the dragon."

"Evander doesn't seem so bad, now that I'm getting to know him." Clarissa couldn't keep a hint of a laugh from her voice at that.

As he had promised the night they'd met, Dorrian had been happy to fill her in on all of Evander's flaws— from his messiness to his hoarding—while the dragon had huffily rolled his eyes and teased right back.

She leaned into Dorrian's hand, smiling up at him. "You aren't so bad now that I've gotten to know you either."

He tugged her closer still. "Then it wouldn't be so bad if I kissed you, would it?"

"Not at all."

With that invitation, Dorrian leaned in and kissed her.

Clarissa's knees wobbled, and she gripped the front of his tunic, warm all the way to her toes

"Dorrian!" Clarissa's sisters squealed as they hugged Dorrian the moment he and Clarissa stepped into the family home in Thysia.

"Shh. You must be quiet, girls," Mama chided quietly as she hefted a sack from the table.

Clarissa couldn't help but smile at how much her sisters had embraced Dorrian as a big brother—the first and currently only brother her sisters had—in the time since she and Dorrian had begun secretly visiting.

It had taken lots of visits and patience, but her

family had come around. Now, they were packing up to leave Thysia tonight, moving to their new home in the Fae Realm.

Clarissa stepped forward and took the sack from her mama. She held open her magical pocket, then slid the sack inside. The sack didn't seem to get smaller, and the pocket didn't appear any larger, but somehow the sack fit through the small pocket opening.

Mama's eyes were wide, but she didn't freak out the way she might have months ago.

Clarissa stepped forward and hugged her mama. "Thank you for trusting me enough to make such a drastic move. The Greater Realm is strange but wonderful."

Mama nodded, her arms tight around Clarissa. "After we realized the truth, we couldn't stay here."

Clarissa's bapi stepped into the room from the back room, carrying an even larger sack. He must have heard that last bit for he nodded to Dorrian before he swept a glance over Clarissa's three younger sisters.

They were the reason, more than anything, that Clarissa's parents were making this move. Their daughters would be safer in the Greater Realm with the dragon than staying here in Thysia as long as it was ruled by the current village elders.

Dorrian strode forward, took the sack from Bapi, and stuffed it into his magical pocket. "If everyone is ready, we should go. Some of the neighbors are waking."

Bapi nodded. Then he herded all of them out of the house. He and Mama were the last to leave, taking one last look around before snuffing out the candle and stepping outside. A single tear trickled down Mama's cheek, but she put her back to the house and strode into the darkness of Thysia's nighttime streets.

Clarissa gave her mama another side hug before she joined Dorrian leading the way through the streets. Her family was giving up so much to leave Thysia and join her in the Greater Realm.

As they left Thysia behind, Clarissa glanced back one last time. She'd debated long and hard on her visits about whether she should tell her friend Nessa that she was alive.

But Nessa's parents wouldn't leave the olive grove the way Clarissa's parents were willing to leave their olive press behind. Nessa would stay in Thysia, and as long as she was there, she would be in danger from the village elders. Knowing Clarissa was alive—knowing the truth of the dragon—would only put her in more danger.

But Clarissa's heart ached, knowing that she was leaving her friend in such danger. Until the sacrifices were ended for good, there was nothing more she could do besides hope.

Epilogue

Dorrian held his daughter, rocking her back and forth to soothe her while Clarissa prepared breakfast.

His wife. His daughter. How full of family and friends his life had become.

"Did Evander say when he'd be coming today?" Clarissa stirred the green eggs, scrambling them in the pan. She didn't even side-eye the food like she used to.

"No. Just that he would be. Probably another report on the current maiden." Dorrian made a face down at Nessa, tickling her tummy. "Your papa's dragon boss is utterly helpless without him. Yes, he is."

The baby giggled, pumped her little legs, and waved her tiny fists.

With Nessa a newborn, Evander had ordered Dorrian to stay home in his and Clarissa's little cottage in the fae village for this time around. Dorrian didn't mind the leave of absence, even if it meant he would have that much more work to do when he returned.

Evander's study would be utterly trashed without him there to oversee things.

"Breakfast is ready." Clarissa set the plates on the table, then took a seat.

Dorrian sat across from her at the table, still holding baby Nessa so that Clarissa could have both hands free to more easily eat her breakfast.

Once she was finished, Clarissa took the baby and retreated to the couch to feed her. Dorrian finished his breakfast now that he had both hands available, then cleaned up the table and the cookware. All he had to do was stack the dishes and pots in a cupboard. When that cupboard was opened again, everything would be sparkling clean.

As he was finishing up, a knock came from the door. "That must be Evander."

"I'll get it." Clarissa tucked Nessa against her shoulder, then hurried to the door, opening it.

The open door blocked Dorrian's view of her and whoever was standing on the doorstep. But after a heartbeat, Clarissa shrieked, "Nessa!"

Dorrian whirled and rushed toward the door, his heart hammering in his throat. But he'd gone no more than two steps when he got a view of the open doorway.

Clarissa was hugging a young woman with dark brown hair, the two of them talking rapidly and smiling. Evander stood at the base of the doorstep, watching Clarissa and the young woman with a smile of his own.

Dorrian halted, sucking in a deep breath as he tried to still his heart. That shriek had been in joy, not terror. His baby was safe.

Did that mean this young woman was Nessa? The

full-grown Nessa for whom his child was named?

Dorrian rested a hand on Clarissa just as she looked over her shoulder at him, so much joy beaming in her smile and sparkling in her eyes. "This is Dorrian, my husband."

"And my real steward." Evander met Dorrian's gaze over the head of the young woman, a chuckle in his voice.

Ah. The young woman—Nessa, presumably—must have lit the candle the night before. Evander was too relaxed in her presence and telling too many truths.

Though there was something in the way Evander looked at Nessa when he turned his gaze back to her, stepping up behind her on the stoop. Dorrian had never seen Evander quite so *himself* with any of the other maidens.

"Then my holiday is at an end?" Dorrian heaved an exaggerated sigh. "And here I was just getting used to kicking up my heels and bothering my wife all day."

He wasn't entirely joking on that. It had been rather nice to spend extra time with Clarissa and their newborn for these past few weeks.

"You were hardly on holiday, busy as you've been in the village." Evander clapped Dorrian on the shoulder, that grin still easy and wide on his face. "If you have a moment, I'd like to get caught up."

Dorrian nodded. He had a great deal to report, since Evander hadn't been as regular in checking in as he usually was. Another interesting point to add to the list Dorrian was building in his mind.

He pressed a kiss to Clarissa's temple. "We'll leave the two of you to talk."

Clarissa sent him a smile and nodded, a hint of joyful tears in her eyes.

Dorrian strode around Clarissa, then joined Evander. Dorrian waited until they had strolled several paces away from the house before he asked in a quiet voice, "So that's Nessa, I take it? My baby's namesake."

Evander nodded. "She's the most recent sacrifice."

"And you didn't think to mention her earlier? Let us know she was here?" Dorrian worked to keep his expression stern.

"I couldn't be sure she was Clarissa's Nessa. I don't know how many girls named Nessa there might be in a village the size of Thysia." Evander shrugged, though his eyes were regretful. "Besides, Clarissa would have wanted to see her as soon as possible, and I didn't want to bring Nessa to see her until she would react well to seeing her friend alive. If Nessa hadn't been ready, Clarissa would've had to watch her words, not knowing how much Nessa knew or how much she should say."

A wise precaution, perhaps, considering how the families of the sacrificed usually reacted to seeing their daughter alive.

Dorrian studied Evander, picking up the note in Evander's voice when he spoke about Nessa.

There was something there. Something Dorrian had never heard from his friend before. As if, for the first time, Evander found himself falling for one of the sacrificed maidens.

Good for him. Dorrian would do everything he could to nudge Evander along. They all knew Evander wouldn't get the thoughts of romance through his thick skull without a little help in the right direction.

The Dragon

These are more snapshots than full stories. Enjoy a few glimpses into Evander's head and his past.

The Beginning

Evander could barely stand still as his papa pointed at the map spread out on the desk in his study. Piles of paperwork had been shoved aside. Some had even fallen to the floor, but his papa's steward wasn't here at the moment to sigh at the treatment of the papers.

"Now that you have come of age, I have secured the blessing of Flight Clawstone to grant you this mountain for your own eyrie." Papa pointed at the spot on the map. "Preliminary surveys have concluded that this mountain is rich in gems. We've had to fend off Flight Icewing several times from claiming it as their territory, so keep a wary eye out."

Evander nodded, trying to tamp down his excitement. It was a big step in a dragon's life to be given a mountain to establish his own eyrie. He would not let down his papa or Flight Clawstone.

Evander soared over the mountain, taking in the small fae village that clustered in a valley below. A clan of gnomes had volunteered to come with him from his papa and mama's eyrie, and they were hard at work carving out the first few tunnels for his eyrie.

He let the mountain winds carry him farther as he took in the land spreading out from his new mountain.

As he drifted over a stand of evergreens, a shiver passed over his scales, so slight that it seemed nothing more than a hint of turbulence.

After a few moments, though, the land beneath him changed. The snow and deep evergreens had changed to something drier, more brown and lighter green.

Strange. Even more strange as dusty brown buildings came into view.

Little did he know at that moment that he was about to make the biggest mistake of his life.

They'd killed her. Evander shook so hard that he could barely keep flying, the mountains before him blurring. He'd returned the frightened girl to her home, and her village had killed her.

The spires of his parents' eyrie rose against the deep blue of the night sky. Evander swooped lower, then landed in an ungainly heap on the balcony. Shifting back into his fae form, he stumbled across the balcony, threw open the doors to the eyrie, and all but fell into his mama's hug, her eyes wide and startled.

She patted his back. "What is wrong, dear?"

For a long moment, Evander just hugged his mama, trying to gather the words to speak. When he did, he glanced from his mama to his papa. "I've made a horrible mistake."

Phoebe

The girl lay on the stone, so still that she looked dead. Evander hurried forward, heart in his throat, but he halted as he saw the rise and fall of her chest.

Not dead, then. That was his worst fear: that he would arrive at the stone only to find that the girl had died before he could rescue her.

The crashing of his footsteps through the snow must have alerted her, but she reacted no more than with a hitch to her breathing. When she spoke, there was a heavy emptiness to her voice. "If that is you, Dragon, please kill me quickly."

Evander crept closer, though he stayed far enough away that he wasn't looming over her. "I'm not going to hurt you. Or eat you. Or whatever you've been told."

In the faint starlight, he couldn't be sure, but she appeared several years older than him. Nearing thirty by human years, if he were to guess. She was on the older end of ages that the village usually sacrificed.

She heaved a sigh, sagging still further against the stone in a way that was too resigned to be relief. Her long brown hair straggled around her, freezing to the stone. "It wouldn't matter if you did kill me. And don't bother asking about my family. They are all dead. There is no one else for you to carry off."

Evander didn't know what to do with that. Most of the girls were terrified because they didn't want to die.

Yet this girl almost seemed like she wanted to die, and that scared him far more than anything else.

"I'm so sorry you lost your family." It must have been recent, given the despair in her voice. He edged closer. "But your life is still worth living. You are still worth it."

She just gave a slight shrug, her face tilted away from him. Despite her despair, she still wasn't looking at his face. She still cared enough for her village to avoid looking at his face.

"I'm going to cut you free." He drew a knife from his magical pocket. There was no need to ask this particular maiden to hold still.

He sawed through the ropes, yet the maiden didn't move.

"I'm going to pick you up now, all right?" Evander kept his voice low and soft.

After a long moment, she gave a tiny nod.

He scooped her up in his arms. Even after doing this many times over the past few years, it was still odd to pick up the maidens like this, so familiarly, cradling them to his chest, when he didn't even know their names yet.

Gathering himself, he launched himself into the sky.

In his arms, the young woman shivered, curling in on herself.

One of these days, he needed to remember to take a blanket along. The more times the village elders left sacrifices in that faerie circle and the more times he visited, the more tied the faerie circle became to the Court of Stone. It was far colder and more wintry than it had been for the first few maidens.

"What's your name?"

After a long moment, she murmured, "Phoebe."

HE STOOD in the doorway as Phoebe sat on her bed, facing him. She held the unlit candle in one hand, a striker in the other. After nearly two months in his eyrie, she was finally regaining some life to her eyes, even if it was difficult to see in the near darkness of the room.

"Please tell me one last time. Nothing is going to happen to the village if I light this candle."

"I'm not going to burn the village, the olive trees, or any of the people. Or kill anyone in any other ways." Evander crossed his arms, leaning against the door jamb. He was barely more than a teenager in dragon years, and already he was so weary, so burdened by all of this. His parents helped where they could, but this was his problem to solve. He studied Phoebe as much as he could in the darkness. "Why do you care about the village so much? They sacrificed you to a dragon. I'm not going to eat you, but they didn't know that."

Phoebe stared at the unlit candle in her hand for a

moment before she sighed. "Perhaps. But there are many people in Thysia who are as scared as I was. They are simply trying to survive. Yes, they should gather their courage to take a stand against the village elders. It is wrong for them to participate, even if they are not the perpetrators. But they are also victims, even if they don't realize it yet."

With that, she worked the striker and lit the candle.

As the light fell on his face, she flinched, but she didn't look away.

THE NEXT MORNING after he had told Phoebe everything, she faced him across the table in the little kitchen nook the gnomes had carved into the stone. He wasn't sure why they had bothered. Meals were haphazard, at best. He really should hire a cook one of these days.

Phoebe's eyes held a glint to them that he'd never seen in her before. "I'd like to help."

"Help?" Evander sank onto one of the chairs.

"Help with the sacrificed maidens. Help with meals and running the eyrie." Phoebe rested her palms on the table. "I'd like to stay here in the eyrie. I have no family. Nowhere else to go. But you desperately need the help."

"Is it that obvious?" Evander couldn't help the lopsided smile.

"Yes." Phoebe didn't smile, but there was the hint that perhaps she could, someday, lingering at the corners of her mouth.

The Stabbing

As Evander sliced through the ropes binding the girl's feet to the stone, she lay tensely still. He moved to her hands, cutting through the ropes.

As soon as her hands were free, she tucked them beneath the folds of her purple dress. Probably seeking warmth.

"Are you—" Evander leaned over her, preparing to help her sit up.

She whipped something out from under her skirt, then swung at him.

Pain flared, and he gasped, staring down at the knife sticking out of his chest, held in a small hand.

She'd stabbed him. None of the maidens had stabbed him before, though a few had attacked him with their fists.

Almost by instinct, he wrapped his own hand over hers, stopping her from yanking out the knife to stab him again.

She gave a scream and yanked, causing more agony to flare through him as the knife wiggled in his chest. When she couldn't withdraw her knife, she beat at him with her other fist.

The part of him that was shaking with pain wanted to shove her away, take off, and leave the crazy young woman to the wolves.

But he couldn't do that. She would die here in the forest with nothing but a knife to defend her.

Instead of shoving her away, he wrapped his other arm around her, doing his best to pin her arms to her sides. Gritting his teeth, he launched the two of them into the air.

Each beat of his wings tore through his chest as the knife shifted. Something warm and wet dribbled against his skin, soaking his shirt. He was probably bleeding all over the girl.

Not that she seemed to notice. She was wriggling and screaming, still trying to yank the knife free, as if she still planned to stab him again despite the fact that they were now high in the air.

Somehow, he managed to keep his wings beating, despite his head going light, his gaze blurring. His stomach churned, and he wasn't sure if he was going to pass out or throw up first.

During their flight, the girl eventually stopped screaming, though he couldn't have said when. She still periodically flailed and wiggled, hissing and spitting like a cat determined to get her claws into him.

Finally, he all but dropped through the opening by the waterfall, landing heavily. Only some depth of determination kept him from falling to his knees right then and there. His grip on the girl loosened just enough that she managed to get one arm free. She dug her fingers into his hair and yanked.

His eyes teared up, and he wasn't sure why his body even bothered registering the additional pain with the agony already coursing through him.

He staggered into the tunnel, half-carrying, half-dragging the girl with him. His gaze was growing black around the edges, and it was all he could do to fumble his way down the passageways until he reached the room at the far end.

He shoved the girl inside and slammed the door closed. This particular door didn't have a lock on the outside. None of the doors did, but this one especially didn't. The maidens weren't prisoners and weren't to be locked inside.

Except that this girl was too dangerous to leave wandering loose. She might attack one of the others who lived in the mountain.

With his head so light he swayed on his feet, he drew in as deep a breath as he could manage and blew a small stream of fire at the latch, melting the metal.

That would hold her. At least until he could send Phoebe and a guard to look after her.

With one hand braced against the wall to stay upright and the other pressed to his chest beside the knife still sticking in him, he tottered back the way he'd come, turning into the tunnel to the kitchens.

As he staggered inside, both Dorrian and Phoebe shot to their feet from where they had been sitting beside the table, waiting for him to return.

"I think I've been stabbed." Evander tried to take one more step.

Then he was on his knees, and he couldn't remember getting there.

Dorrian appeared at his side, gripping his shoulder. "Clearly. What happened? No, don't answer that. Doesn't matter. You need the healer."

Evander gazed down at himself. Blood soaked the front of his shirt and his breeches all the way to his knees. That was a lot of blood. He must have bled all over the poor girl. "I must have bled on her. Phoebe, you'll need to look after her. But take a guard. She's a little vicious."

Dorrian was saying something, but Evander couldn't hear him past a strange rushing in his ears.

And then, he passed out.

EVANDER PEELED OPEN his gummy eyes, blinking up at the curved, stone ceiling. Light streamed through the windows beside his bed, pooling deep orange against the wall as it did at sunset.

A scuff drew his gaze to the other side of his room, where Dorrian paced before the fireplace that Evander never lit. Dorrian's steps were stilted, almost violent, as he stomped back and forth, his hands clasped behind his back.

Evander pushed to sit up, but pain flared through his chest. He pressed a hand to his chest, grimacing at the pain.

How injured had he been, if he was still in this much

pain? As a Greater Dragon, he healed faster than other fae.

Dorrian spun to him, his jaw set. He wagged his finger at Evander. "Do you know how long you've been out?"

"No. I've been unconscious." Evander gritted his teeth and shifted enough that he could lean against the headboard.

"Exactly! You've been out for hours! Phoebe and I have been worried sick!" Dorrian marched closer, still waving that stern finger. "What were you thinking?"

"It wasn't like I asked to be stabbed." Evander forced himself to draw in a deep breath, despite the pain. "How is the girl?"

"Feral, as far as we can tell." Dorrian halted next to the bed and crossed his arms, still glaring. "She's not the one who flew across realms bleeding out with a knife in his chest."

Evander huffed, then grimaced at the pain. Being stabbed was no laughing matter.

EVANDER STOOD at the end of the corridor, glancing down the passageway at the door at the far end. Light blazed from beneath the door. That was an interesting twist, on top of this girl stabbing him. Apparently she had chosen violence that morning.

Next to him, Dorrian had his arms crossed tightly. "I don't think you should go in there alone."

"I'll be fine. I'm a dragon." Evander shifted, his teeth sharpening in his mouth, his wings rising from his back.

The process didn't hurt, but it still sent an uncomfortable sensation—almost like a dizzy nausea—through him before he settled into his half-dragon shape.

"She stabbed you once before." Dorrian's scowl deepened.

"And I'll be more wary now. I doubt she has another weapon." Those filmy dresses the maidens were forced to wear were hardly designed for concealing weapons. He was rather surprised she'd even managed to hide the one knife.

Dorrian huffed a breath and shook his head. "Fine. Go get yourself stabbed again. I'll have the village healer waiting."

Evander rolled his eyes at Dorrian's dramatics, then pushed away from the wall. His head was still swirly after losing so much blood, but he wasn't about to admit that. This maiden had been left locked in her room like a prisoner for far too long as it was. Under guard, Phoebe had seen to it that she was given food and water to wash up. But that was all the care she had been given.

The latch had been replaced, and a new lock now graced the outside of the door.

Gathering the rest of his strength, Evander knocked on the door. "May I come in? It is the dragon."

Normally, he didn't have to clarify that. But given this girl's state of mind, he wanted her to know who she might be letting in.

A moment of silence, then the girl spoke, her voice hard with determination. "Come in, dragon."

Evander slid the locking bolt free, then pushed the door open.

The girl stood beside the bed, her back to the wall,

gripping the fireplace poker. She still wore the purple dress, bloodstains and all, her brown hair straggling over her shoulders.

Candles blazed on the bedside table, the floor between them, along the fireplace mantel, and pretty much every surface in the room. How the girl had managed to find so many candles, he didn't know. Perhaps she had figured out how to get the wardrobe or the magical pocket that would be in the dress in the wardrobe to supply her with them.

She gazed straight at his face without flinching, the fire of defiance in her eyes. "So you didn't die."

"Sorry to disappoint you." Evander leaned against the door behind him, not wanting to admit how much his legs were growing weak from standing so long. "Aren't you worried that I'll burn the village down?"

"Go ahead." She gripped the poker tighter, raising it slightly. "I'll help, if you like."

Beneath the fire of defiance in her eyes, there were layers of pain that he didn't think only came from being sacrificed the night before. But he wasn't going to ask. It was the type of pain she would only share with someone she trusted, and that certainly wasn't him.

"Sorry to disappoint you twice in one day, but I'm not going to burn the village." Evander leaned even more heavily against the door. Sitting down sounded really good, but he didn't dare relax that much around her.

At least her defiance meant that he was spared the usual weeks of tiptoeing around the truth until she was ready to open her eyes. Her eyes were open, and she was already staring at him. She could handle the truth.

"I never wanted the sacrifices." Evander held the girl's gaze, hoping she'd hear the truth in his words. "I would never burn the village down. I don't eat any of the maidens. That is all a myth created by the village elders over the years."

For a long moment, the girl stared at him, blinking. Then something in her expression changed, an echo of that pain and anger still in her eyes. "I should have known. Those lying…" She broke into a string of swear words that would have made Evander's mama tan his scaly dragon hide if he'd uttered them growing up.

Not that he could blame her for the language any more than he blamed her for stabbing him.

Eventually, she wound her tirade down. As she stopped speaking, she drew in a deep breath, releasing it slowly as if gathering herself. After setting the poker down, she faced Evander as if seeing him for the first time. "If what you say is true, then I'm sorry for stabbing you."

"I don't blame you." Evander finally let himself slide down the door to sit on the floor.

The girl sat on the bed, smoothing her stained skirts. "Why don't you explain what is truly going on?"

Evander did so, keeping his story as succinct as possible since all he wanted to do was climb back into bed and sleep. Getting stabbed sure did a number on him, even as a dragon.

Once he had finished, the girl was quiet for a long moment. Then she fisted her hands around one of the bloodstains in her skirt. "What happens to me now? I'm not going back there."

"Obviously. They'd kill you." Evander opened his

mouth, then paused. Normally, this was the point he'd offer the sacrificed maiden either a home in the fae village or a home in one of the human villages on the far side of the mountain.

But this particular girl didn't seem a good fit for either of those options.

Instead, he asked, "Do you have any family back in Thysia?"

"No." The girl's tone was short. Hard. "I leave no one behind."

Again, he wasn't going to ask. That would be something for someone else to help her heal from.

"There's a court here in the Fae Realm, the Court of Swordmaidens." Evander met her gaze, seeing the interest there. "The court doesn't allow men. Only women. They train to fight, and they are known as some of the best warriors in all of the Fae Realm."

Her eyes lit as she leaned forward. "Does this court allow humans?"

"Yes. The Court of Swordmaidens is open to any woman." Evander found himself smiling at the eagerness in her voice and eyes. She would do well in the Court of Swordmaidens. She was certainly stabby enough.

Stealing from the Dragon

Evander stood at one of the windows in his study, watching the trail down the mountain.

Dorrian burst into the study. "The maiden! She—"

"I know." Evander gestured out the window. The most recent maiden was disappearing into the gloom beneath the evening trees, hiking as quickly as she could. "Boss Gob informed me that she filled her pocket with gems."

Which was a more substantial amount than it seemed, since she was wearing a dress supplied by the wardrobe and thus had a magical pocket.

"Should we stop her?" Dorrian gestured, as if he wasn't sure what to do.

Evander stuffed down that fiery, itchy feeling inside him. She was stealing from *his* mountain. The dragon in him wanted to swoop down there and demand the return of his gems.

But the gems weren't his. They weren't a part of his

hoard. They were destined for other courts in the Fae Realm. More than that, he would have given the gems to her, had she but asked.

"No. She was clever enough to figure out the magical pockets and how to steal the gems." Evander turned away from the window. "But we're going to secretly guard her and help her get back into the Human Realm. I suspect that if she was clever enough to pull this much off, she will be cautious when returning to her family."

Dorrian sighed, then nodded. "I'll get food from Phoebe, then set out. You'd better fly ahead and shadow her from above."

A sound plan. Evander pushed open one of the windows—one of the few that opened in this mountain eyrie—and flung himself into the air.

As he fell, he shifted, his wings rising from his back and snapping open. His wings caught the wind, and he soared higher and higher until the girl was no more than a speck far below. With her human eyesight, she wouldn't be able to tell him apart from a large bird, especially against the darkness of the night sky.

AT THE FAERIE CIRCLE, Evander went ahead of her and did his best to tug the magic to lead her through the barrier between the realms without her figuring out what was happening. What he'd done must have worked, for she stumbled out the other side, reaching the stone altar set among the evergreens.

At the other side, she hurried down the mountain

path as quickly as possible, glancing around as if looking for wolves.

Evander lingered in the trees, waiting for Dorrian. His presence kept the wolves from coming anywhere near.

Dorrian stumbled between the trees, halting next to Evander. "That was a long walk."

"We can fly on the way back." Evander shrugged and set out again. They had probably given the girl enough of a head start.

"I'm not getting carried back like a damsel in your arms." Dorrian fell into step after him.

"I'll turn into a full dragon, and you can ride on my back." Evander preferred not to be ridden like an animal, but he would make an exception in this case.

"I suppose." Dorrian still sounded put out, even though he wasn't the one offering to be a beast of burden.

In Thysia, they quieted. Evander sniffed, trailing her scent to a home that had a light beaming from a window.

Even as he and Dorrian settled into a dark alley across the way, someone yanked all the shutters closed. Moments later, even the light beneath the door was snuffed out.

The girl's family must have been just as clever and practical as she was. For a mere two hours after their daughter had returned to them, alive and well and carrying a pocketful of gems, the entire family had packed up and was on the road, headed for the seaside.

Evander and Dorrian trailed them through the night and into the morning. At a seaside city, the girl and her family bartered for transport on one of the many wooden vessels at the docks.

"Well, that's that." Dorrian dusted off his hands on his tunic. "That's one maiden we won't have to worry about."

No, this particular maiden would be fine. If she and her family were smart, they'd dole out those gems wisely. Given their reactions so far, he had no fears for them.

Once it was night, Evander retreated outside of the city and transformed into a dragon. He swung his head to Dorrian as he lowered himself to the ground as much as he could. "Climb on."

Dorrian grimaced. "Don't you have a saddle or something?"

"Of course not. I'm not a horse." Evander bumped Dorrian with his nose.

Dorrian swatted his nose. "You're a huge dragon. Far worse."

"Do you want to walk all the way back?" Evander puffed some smoke at Dorrian. Flying wasn't that bad.

"No." Dorrian sighed, then clambered up Evander's leg. He settled himself on Evander's neck just before his shoulders, gripping one of the spikes that ran down his back.

Evander rose to his full height, and Dorrian made a sound as he hugged Evander's neck.

As Evander launched himself into the sky, Dorrian shouted, "I'm getting you a saddle!"

Nessa

The girl had her eyes squeezed closed as she lay there, tensed and still on the stone. But instead of a scream or tears, what came out of her mouth instead was, "If you're going to eat me, please eat me whole. Or kill me quickly first."

It was said with such an underlying layer of snark beneath the veiling fear that Evander nearly snorted a laugh. The snarky ones were so much better than the tearful maidens. "I'm not going to eat you. I find maidens are far too stringy for my taste. I prefer a good rack of lamb slow roasted over a fire."

He shouldn't have said it. He should have stuck with calmly reassuring. But it was too irresistible to match her hint of sarcasm with some humor of his own.

She didn't burst into tears. While she kept her eyes closed, her mouth pursed. "Then why don't you require sheep for the sacrifice instead of a maiden, if you like roast lamb so much?"

Asking the hard questions already. He had a feeling he was going to like this particular maiden.

EVANDER CRADLED Nessa in his arms, ignoring the attempts of the stone gremlins to claw him with their pincers. His heart beat harder, not at the minuscule annoyance of the stone gremlins but at the feel of her in his arms.

Spending the day with her, sharing gyros and sneezing over parchments, must have gone to his head. He had never enjoyed spending time with any of the sacrificed maidens the way he did Nessa.

It almost made him want...

But no. She was his captive. Here because her village sacrificed her. He would not take advantage of that. Doing anything else would be dishonorable.

EVANDER STRODE INTO THE STUDY, his heart light, his head still swirling as if he was still soaring through the clouds.

Nessa had kissed him. She'd kissed him and she loved him and it was all he could do to stroll normally and not turn into a dragon so he could roar his joy to the sky.

As the door swung shut behind him, Dorrian glanced up. His expression must have been particularly mushy, for Dorrian smirked, set down his pen, and leaned back in the chair. "A good day?"

"Yes." Evander's face hurt from smiling. "I'm going to marry Nessa."

"Good. You finally got that sorted." Dorrian laced his hands behind his head.

"And we know how to end the sacrifices." Evander could hardly believe those words were coming out of his mouth.

"What?" The smirk dropped from Dorrian's face as he sat up straight again.

"It is Nessa's idea. We need to have a meeting to discuss the details, but Nessa and I came up with a rough plan." Evander paused, then choked out the next words. "I'm…I'm going to need a saddle."

"Ha! Yes!" Dorrian shot to his feet, then reached into his pocket. He fished around for a moment, then yanked something large and leather out. He plopped it onto the desk with a creak of leather and clunk of buckles.

Evander stared down at it, grimacing. He could already picture the itchy, constricting thing buckled onto his dragon back. "You carry a dragon saddle around in your pocket."

"Yep. You know how I like to be prepared." Dorrian crossed his arms. "And I was never flying again without a saddle."

Evander scowled and resisted the urge to shudder. But to end the sacrifices, he'd do whatever it took.

Even wear a saddle.

EVANDER STOOD to the side of the large room, just taking it in. All of the tables and benches were packed, both with fae and with all of the sacrificed maidens who had remained in the Fae Realm. A few of those who had moved to the human villages on the far side of the mountain had even made the arduous trip to come to this celebration.

Nessa, wearing that dark purple dress again, though the tiara and jeweled collar had been returned to his mother, mingled with the guests, her cheeks flushed as if she was embarrassed to receive so much praise and attention.

But she was the woman of the hour, having ended Thysia's sacrifices once and for all.

Phoebe halted next to him and held out a plate. "You shouldn't look so melancholy. This is a celebration."

"I know. And I'm not." Evander took the plate, but for once he didn't immediately reach for the food on it, his thoughts too full to listen to the complaints of his stomach. "I just can't believe the sacrifices are over. After all this time."

"I understand. It's hard to comprehend." Phoebe stared off into the room, though she didn't appear to be taking in the party.

Something in Evander's chest sank as he took in her somber expression. In that moment, she looked so much like the hopeless young woman she'd been all those years ago. "Do you ever regret never marrying and settling down as so many of the others did? You gave up so much to stay here and help me and all the other maidens who came after you."

Phoebe tilted her head, considering his words for a long moment. Then she shook her head. "No, I don't regret it. Not one bit. There were moments when I would wonder if, perhaps, I should actually think about marrying. But then another maiden would be sacrificed. Or you'd bring home someone like Dorrian or Daphne who needed looking after. And I'd find myself with so much work for my hands—so much care for my heart—that I never felt the need to seek anything else."

"The sacrifices are over. You are free to leave and find a life for yourself, if you wish." Even as he said the words, Evander's heart hurt at the thought of losing Phoebe. She had become a friend, almost another mother figure, during the long years. He couldn't imagine the eyrie without her.

"You aren't getting rid of me that easily." Phoebe smiled, shaking her head again. "The sacrifices are over, but there is still plenty for me to do here. All of you still need looking after. There is still the ongoing healing for those who have been sacrificed. Then there's Dorrian's and Clarissa's child and any children you and Nessa eventually have. While I might not have what most would call a family of my own, my life is and will be far from empty or unfulfilled."

Evander wasn't sure what to say to that. All he could do was dip his head and force out a rough, "Thank you."

Phoebe patted his arm. Then she strode off, smiling, as she joined the celebration to mark the end of the sacrifices.

After a few moments, Nessa drifted from the party to join him. She laced her fingers with his. "Is something wrong? You aren't snacking."

"Nothing's wrong." Evander set the plate on the nearest table, the better to draw Nessa into his arms.

"Just appreciating how fortunate I am to have you in my life."

Nessa grinned, wrapping her arms around his neck. "Very fortunate."

Holding her close, he kissed her. No eyrie, no gem, no hoard could ever compare to the woman he held in his arms.

Also by Tara Grayce

World of Elven Alliance / Alliance Kingdoms

ELVEN ALLIANCE

Fierce Heart

War Bound

Death Wind

Troll Queen

Pretense

Shield Band

Elf Prince

Heart Bond

Elf King

WAR OF THE ALLIANCE

Wings of War

Stalk the Sky

Fly to Fury

Tales of the Fae Realm

COURT OF MIDSUMMER MAYHEM

Stolen Midsummer Bride

Steal a Swordmaiden's Heart

Forest of Scarlet

Wild Fae Primrose

Night of Secrets

A VILLAIN'S EVER AFTER

Bluebeard and the Outlaw

SACRIFICED HEARTS

Mountain of Dragons and Sacrifice

Of Dragons and Stone

TETHERED HEARTS

Ties of Bargains

Middle Grade

PRINCESS BY NIGHT

Lost in Averell

Acknowledgments

Thanks so much for reading *Of Dragons and Stone*! I hope you enjoyed a little extra glimpse into the world of *Mountain of Dragons and Sacrifice*. If you loved the book, please consider leaving a review on Amazon or Goodreads. Reviews help your fellow readers find books that they will love.

If you ever find typos in my books, feel free to message me on social media or send me an email through the Contact Me page of my website.

If you want to learn about all my upcoming releases, get great book recommendations, and see a behind-the-scenes glimpse into the writing process, sign up for my newsletter at www.taragrayce.com.

Thanks so all my family and friends! You guys make this crazy writing life possible and you are the best in so many unique ways!

Thank you to my proofreaders Mindy and Deborah, who worked this freebie into their schedules, despite my propensity to write bonus books and add to their work.

Made in the USA
Columbia, SC
28 January 2025

52340445R00079